The Decline of Pigeons

The Decline of Pigeons

Janice Deal

Queen's Ferry Press

Queen's Ferry Press
8240 Preston Road
Suite 125-151
Plano, TX 75024
www.queensferrypress.com

Published 2013 by Queen's Ferry Press

Cover art by Anna Jóelsdóttir; *on blueberry hill* (Acrylic, ink, fabric, thread on drafting film on wood structure. 2012 [detail].) Courtesy of the artist and Stux Gallery, NY.

Cover design by John Hensler

First edition July 2013

ISBN 978-1-938466-09-0

Printed in the United States of America

Praise for
The Decline of Pigeons:

"The nine unblinkingly truthful stories in Janice Deal's debut collection, *The Decline of Pigeons*, are layered with tragedy, guilt, desperation, and betrayal. Emotionally engaging and entertaining, these stories are told with a gentle precision that elegantly explores the characters' experiences with domestic strife, amputation, broken dreams, and death. Whether describing parents' failed connections with siblings, sisters who can't agree, or relationships with a repo man and a husband who speaks to God, this collection endears itself to the reader with insights that illuminate what ties these stories together: the inevitability of loss."

 —Jason Lee Brown, Series Editor for *New Stories from the Midwest*

"In *The Decline of Pigeons*, Janice Deal leads us deep into the heart of human nature to reveal the turmoil, self-delusion, and moments of unexpected clarity that accompany profound loss. I love these characters—flawed, real, and marked by compassion. And I love Deal's voice: arresting, brave, uniquely her own. I will return to this book again and again, for the joy and sense of solace it brings me."

 —Katherine Shonk, author of *Happy Now?*

"Janice Deal's collection of stories demands your attention right from the first sharp, glorious sentences to the last poignant moment ending the stories of these men and women just on the edge of society living quiet, intense lives. Old men who can't quite connect, women who risk love in order to find something better, people who are like us . . . and nothing like us. They bare their souls with an honesty that is both raw and heartening as we meet them at moments filled with the mundane that turn explosive. You can't help but let them burrow into your consciousness, becoming more complex well after you've read the last page."

—Jill Pollack, director of StoryStudio Chicago

"Bright flashes of beauty and wit stream through Janice Deal's elegant stories, as the characters repeatedly try to maintain their poise in the face of unexpected obstacles and threats. Her mastery of form and technique arises from a deep understanding of the souls of her characters, and she never flinches from exposing the darkness that underlies their brittle efforts to cope."

—Fred Shafer, literary editor, lecturer, Northwestern University School of Continuing Studies

"Janice Deal renders her characters with a profound humanity. They are ordinary people confronting solitude, alienation, and loss. And they are rare birds, each unique in how they bear their wounds, scars, betrayals, and horror. As Deal trains her unwavering light on them, the reader shares in their pain, wherein lies redemption. These moving and sometimes darkly humorous stories cut straight to my heart, and there they will remain long after turning the last page of this stunning new collection."

—Kevin McCoy, actor, playwright, founder and artistic director, Théâtre Humain

"There are so many things to love about Janice Deal's collection, *The Decline of Pigeons*. I fell for her characters—young mothers, sly grandparents, drifters, accomplices—all hanging on and making do after great loss. I fell for her eye and its uncanny way with the social markers that unite and divide: the pressed-wood furniture, the shirts with pearl-button collars, the owl figurines. But finally, what most astonishes—and delights—is Deal's hard-won knowledge, expressed with such aching beauty, that although connection will wear us down, and wear us out, connect we must."

—James Magruder, author of *Sugarless*

To Mom and Dad

To Marion

To David

Contents

Aurora 15

Nature 37

Six Foot 69

Sailor Lake 89

The Decline of Pigeons in the Natural World 111

Phoenix 139

Darkness Can Fall Without Warning 161

Repo Man 187

Dinosaurs 209

Aurora

Atwater spends close to a week in Chicago before calling his daughter. The other occupants of the men's hotel are *lifers*, *penitents*, he thinks, and he regards them with scorn. Jaws working at curds of tobacco or gum, they shuffle past in the lobby, with its dim gilt and once-grand balustrade. Atwater doesn't use the paneled closet in his room, the way he imagines the other tenants do, nor does he hang his robe on the pale china hook that juts from the bathroom door, a splintered bone; his shirts remain folded, precisely arranged, in his suitcase. During the day, Atwater escapes the hotel and walks the streets named after lakes. He is a lean-hipped man, fit in his middle age, with a small, hard swell of belly, and narrow eyes saved from stoniness by their blue clarity. He glances furtively at his reflection in the shop windows, strutting past tooled shoes, chunky diamonds, massive tweed overcoats defining a winter still months away. It is these last that give him pause. If he means to live here, and he does, he must dress the part.

On his fifth day in the city, he ventures into a store—its giddy heights described by a towering, shining windowfront—and slings a coat over his shoulders. An experiment. The unaccustomed weight is staggering.

It is a relief to emerge into the heat and light again, and without planning to he walks back to the hotel, checks out, hoofs it to Union Station. A couple miles at least but he is from Tennessee, after all; he could hike all day in this humidity, he reminds himself, a fifty-pound pack on his back.

"Princess!" he bellows into a pay phone. "I'm in Chicago. For work." This is almost true. Atwater leans away from the phone to study the hieroglyphics of the train schedule posted behind him, the figures running together, a lurid, digitized green. Trains running all day. "Practically got my ass in your back yard!"

"Chicago and Aurora ain't that close, Daddy," Candace says.

Atwater hears the crack of a match, flaring, and his daughter's sharp inhalation. "Still smokin', heh? Nasty habit, girl." He fumbles in his breast pocket for his own pack.

Mannish, his daughter. But all that could have changed: he hasn't seen Candy in ten, fifteen years.

"How old you now, anyway?" Atwater asks.

"Old enough to know better."

North of thirty, then, Atwater decides.

"Daddy, if you're thinking of coming and staying here, I got no use for you."

"Say, hey there." Atwater laughs. "I just thought you could show me the sights."

"What, that Belle you're living with gone and quit you?"

Behind Atwater, the terminal commences its dull roar: the static, uninflected voice of the intercom; crowd bobbing past.

Candace chuckles. "I thought so," she says. "How'd you get this number anyway?"

"From your little brother." Atwater glances at the white-faced clock on the station wall; the next train out to Aurora leaves in ten minutes.

"I'd like to kill that son of a bitch," Candy says, but her voice sounds fond.

"He's a good boy."

There is a pause, then Candy says, "I thought maybe you were dead."

"Well, I ain't." Atwater turns to watch the passengers entering the terminal. Business people, mostly, but a harassed-looking young woman with a child by the hand stands out in her cheap print dress, her hair slipping free from a loose ponytail. Time was he could charm a woman like that; Atwater straightens the stiff plastic collar on his windbreaker. Oh yeah, he used to turn heads. He winks at the girl and, flustered, she smiles distractedly at him.

"Bye, Daddy," Candace says, and hangs up.

—

Candy had been a solid, humorous baby, her round face marked by a trust so profound it left Atwater dizzy. Like any number of virile, boastful young men, he had thrilled at Karenmary's pregnancy, but nothing had prepared him for how much he would love his daughter: from the moment Candace was hoisted screaming into the world, Atwater recognized himself in her features. The child's forehead, like Atwater's, rose into a pure and narrow dome, crowned by a thicket of hair—a rich, sunny brown. Her nose was straight; she cried, lustily, and upon hearing this

Atwater felt for the first time that the world, with all its glare of light and treachery, might hold a sensible pattern. Candy was a summer baby, but he and his wife were young, and afraid: they bundled her in layers and he held her like a piece of china, each leaf on the sugar maple outside Karenmary's hospital room clear-cut against a sky the color of sorghum.

—

The cab from the train station has no air conditioning, and Atwater shrugs off his windbreaker, cocking his head to catch what breeze there is, yellow and baking, through the open window. "Town looks good," he says, as if he has been to Aurora before, but the cabby, who wears a mesh tractor cap and pressed jeans, drives silently, his small hands quick on the wheel. One eye is almost swollen shut with a wen. "My daughter, she's the one has me visiting north here," Atwater says to the back of the man's head. "I'm gonna surprise her. I don't need to tell a man like you—a girl needs her daddy." The cab driver exhales and Atwater settles back in his seat. "Holy God, she'll be surprised."

Belle *had* kicked him out. From the apartment they'd shared and she'd paid for, with its three rooms and intimate smells: the sweetish perfume Belle wore, and roast pork, and the Norfolk pine kept penned in a wicker basket in the corner. Oh, his daughter got that right, but she'd always been sharp. More so than her brother—poor Raymie, got held back a grade, not that you'd know it now, nosir.

What Atwater needs is a job. Sales, maybe: didn't Karenmary used to tell him he could sweet-talk a zebra into giving up its stripes? Not yet sixty and still in his prime; he'll tell his daughter how he means to get a job. Because he isn't stupid: before he can work he has to have a place to stay, to get on his feet. The men's hotel, it was beneath him. Raymie, back home, doesn't have the room, and Candace can take him in for awhile; hell, he won't stay long, and she's his daughter, for Chrissakes.

When the cab turns into a cluster of small homes—*Maple Acres*, the sign says, and there *are* maples, not saplings, lining streets laid plumb through a farmer's field sometime in Atwater's own lifetime—Atwater pulls out the gas receipt on which he's written Candy's address. His eyes flick between the crabbed numbers on the paper and the houses they pass: Cape Cods, ranches, with carports rather than garages, bass boats canting in their narrow shade. When the car pulls up before a tidy gray ranch, Atwater presses his last twenty into the cabby's hand. "My daughter's house," he says, before the man drives away, his cab farting exhaust.

Squaring his shoulders, Atwater strides up to the front stoop, where a wind chime hangs motionless and the doorbell is an eagle, molded from green copper. It is a fine house, the nicest on the block.

"Candy!" he cries when the front door swings inward. But the woman behind the screen door isn't his daughter. She's a squat woman, closer to Atwater's age, with a creased purse of a face and cropped hair dyed the color of a blood orange.

"Candy ain't here just now. Who wants to know?" The woman squints at him. Arms folded across great, fallen breasts, she makes no move to open the screen.

"It's her daddy, come calling!" Atwater lowers his Samsonite. He had prepared a speech for his daughter. Hell, he *expected* her to bring up certain episodes, that last dinner, for instance; Candy's high school graduation, wasn't it? But what he hadn't bargained for was this, a stranger, her broad toad's face cracked into a grin that stops just beneath the eyes.

The woman stares at the suitcase in its girdle of strapping tape. "I have it Candy don't want nothing to do with you," she says. Her eyes are heavy-lidded. They wink, lazily.

"Who *are* you?" Atwater says. It's hot on the porch, the white cement of the steps bouncing light. Over the woman's shoulder the house is secret as a cave.

"I'm her mother-in-law," the woman says. Atwater passes a hand over his hair, thin at the crown, slick from the heat. Raymie hadn't mentioned anything about a wedding.

"Well, sure you are," he says finally. "You know how these kids can be." He shrugs, raising his hands, palms up.

"She'll be back by and by," the woman replies, making to shut the door. The flesh of her neck, loose and tanned dark as a nut, wobbles when she shakes her head. "She's at work. Come back in a few hours. She can let you in herself, if she has a mind to."

"Wait!" Atwater says. He wants to know where Candy works, but pride holds his tongue. "What's your name?" he asks instead.

"That would be Sherry." The woman raises her eyebrows, which are level and dark, unspoiled by dye. She is a great fist of a woman but she might have been pretty once. Atwater must not underestimate her.

"Cy Atwater," he offers, but she's already closed the door.

———

Just a little glitch, that's all. This person, this *Sherry*, could be an obstacle, no doubt about that, but he can handle her. Once his daughter gets home his real work can begin. Atwater sees this now, hiking out to a convenience mart that he spotted on the cab ride in. The store radiates a dead incandescence of florescent tube lighting, and it's air conditioned to the point of discomfort, but he is soothed by the aisles of food and drink, and empties his pockets to buy two sixers of beer and a turkey sandwich. Atwater sits on the cement stoop outside the plate-glass doors of the store to avoid the frank stare of the teenaged clerk, who fingered the metal stud in her nose as he counted out first bills, then dimes, nickels, and pennies. Atwater unwinds the sandwich from its wad of plastic: five dry bites and it's gone but for the hardest parts of the bread. He tries to make the beer last, sipping it, turning the pages of a paperback, *The Last of the Mohicans*, fished from the inner pocket of his coat.

He used to teach high school English. Years ago, in another lifetime; he was the first in his family to get into and through college, and during the years of his employment his parents and sister said he talked differently. "Show off," they accused. Later he let his speech slip back; it was like a tic you shed but then welcomed for its familiarity, its lack of pretense. But at the time he was married to Karenmary and they had their plans: a house, not unlike Candy's, and soon enough, a child. Atwater thinks about this now, eyes trained on the book's crisp yellow pages. He might remind Candy how he wore a dark tie to work, how the kids they called him sir, even though they were, what? Five years younger than he was? It doesn't matter. He wants his daughter to remember that he's had a place to fall from.

Atwater looks up. Down the asphalt parking lot, two men in sport coats juggle coffee and pastries. A Danish slips and shatters on the pavement, and the men laugh, fat and admirable. When they climb into a sedan unmarked by dirt or rust, a narrow-faced dog appears almost immediately around the end of the strip mall; it gulps at the shreds of pastry, eyes cast up in its head.

Watching the dog crouch and eat, unrepentant, Atwater can still call up the strenuous arc of his teaching years. God Almighty, he'd had his plans. He was drinking then, but had the notion that it only made him garrulous. He wore his hair—dark, plentiful—greased high and fragrant over his forehead, and he fired off jokes, making him a favorite of the students. The principal thought him an ass but kept his own counsel, at least until later; all that was still in the future. That one day there was a party for the teachers and their families, a district-wide affair at a park so ungenerous that its febrile brown grass was baked flat to the ground. The festivities had been going for some time when a dog wandered in, from the playing fields north of the picnic grounds. It was a dark animal, thickly made with a square wet snout worn like a party mask and eyes the crinkled red of currants. Candy had been playing by herself, not fifteen feet from him, three years old then, or four, her cotton dress holding the light. Karenmary was helping with the food; baby Raymie was home with a sitter. And Atwater? He'd been nursing a gin and tonic, cracking wise, one bleary eye on his daughter while the other followed the shapely ass and pert tits of the dark-haired cocktease who taught third grade.

There was something wrong with the dog, the way it ran at an angle, its shoulders and blunt ram of a head slung low: it was sick, or pissed off, or both. It loped close to his daughter, who loved dogs but screamed when she saw this one. Terror made Atwater weightless. He dropped his drink and went running.

"You're lucky," the doctor told him in the ER. He was a

young man, the bridge of his nose tormented by spectacles, and Atwater, who hated the man's dispassionate voice, had an inkling of the gulf that would separate him in the future from people like this. From Karenmary, too, for she had gotten to their daughter first, though Atwater had been closer. Moving with a mother's unerring instinct, she screamed and beat at the dog's back and face even as it took Candy up like a doll in those great hinged jaws. "You probably saved the girl's life," the doctor said to Karenmary, treating her wounds. For as long as the marriage lasted, the marks on Karenmary's arms, their raised, lurid twining, were a mockery of Atwater, of his own impotence and disgrace. His daughter was scarred, too, a great seam coursing down her middle like a zipper, as if stitches were all that were needed to make her whole again.

By all accounts Atwater should have been grateful; he'd come so close, he understood, to losing them both. But in the next few months, he found himself wishing that he'd been the one to take on the dog. Wrestling Candy free might have granted him a useful nobility, for one thing: by then the affair had been discovered, the bills for the motel and sordid boxes of cheap candy, and Karenmary never neglected to remind him when they argued— vicious fights, paced by the crack of flying furniture—that she was the one who'd saved Candy. "Adulterer," she hissed. "Too busy looking for tail to mind your own child. Alcoholic." And though the latter wasn't quite true then, it *was* a few years later, when she left him. By then he'd drunk himself out of his teaching position and into a roundelay of jobs—security guard, janitor, toll collector—that never lasted long enough to make an impression: on himself, on anyone else.

"Damn," Atwater says, watching the sedan pull away and

starting in on another beer. At least he's cut back on his drinking since leaving Belle. No hard stuff, even when he wants it.

People can change. That's what he told Belle, for all the good it did him; he means to have better luck with Candy. Atwater carefully licks his fingers. As soon as the sun sinks to the level of the Carpet Warehouse sign, he lets himself have a smoke.

———

When Atwater returns to his daughter's house it's almost five o'clock but still hot as noonday, sun gilding the windows and granting the little ranch its best face. He hoists his suitcase up the steps.

"You," he says when the door opens. Sherry gazes at him through the screen door. She's changed into a pink tank top with seashells printed across her heavy breasts; fat as a town dog, this one.

"She ain't here yet," Sherry agrees.

"I got me some cold ones," he says, holding up what's left of the beer. Eight bottles swing from his fingers, sweating in the heat. "It's warm enough."

"That it is." Sherry studies him. "I don't go in for that much anymore," she says, nodding at the beer.

"Me neither." Atwater shifts from one foot to the other. He waggles the bottles and they ring like chimes.

Sherry's face takes on a look of decision. "Well, come on in, then," she says. She unlatches the screen and holds it open. "But if Candy wants you out, don't look to me for helping any."

"No, ma'am." Just over the threshold, Atwater sets his suitcase down and tucks the beer into his chest. They are in a small foyer, living room to the left, a pretty jewel box of a space with the bay window. To the right, a boxy dining set—Karenmary's mother's; Atwater remembers its dimpled veneer—overwhelms a tiny dining room. The furniture is carefully tended and grouped, the table topped with an ornate arrangement of spangled fake flowers.

"We'll set out back 'til Candy comes," Sherry says, hustling him straight through the house and out the patio door.

Atwater shades his eyes. Candy's yard is immaculate, almost fussy, its edges drawn by a border of marigolds and a spiky red flower Atwater can't name. Against the house, a stone fountain funnels water in an endless gurgling loop, reminding him that he needs to pee.

"It'll be cooler soon enough," Sherry says. She flops onto a lawn chair with a confidence that verges on gracefulness, gesturing for Atwater to do the same.

The only other chair is canvas; it cradles his ass like a sling. He crosses his legs, but, still disoriented from the heat, uncrosses them after a moment, planting both feet on the patio stones. He cracks open two beers and reaches one out to Sherry. "Just in case you're so inclined," he says.

"Oh, well. All right." She takes a lusty pull then raises the bottle to squint at it. Her expression holds a surprised curiosity. "I keep meaning to quit," she says. "I expect I will when I have to."

"Sweet beer," Atwater says. "Won't hurt us none." The fountain gurgles. He crosses his legs.

"So what do you do with yourself?" Sherry asks.

Atwater takes a sip and holds the bottle against his forehead. His jacket clings to his back, to the wet and salt of his shirt.

"I'm semi-retired at the moment," he says.

Sherry snorts. "I'll bet you are!"

Piss on you, Atwater thinks. He looks away, at the duck lawn ornaments placed with elaborate casualness in the middle of the lawn, bill-to-bill, as if kissing. One, made of cement, wears a removable yellow slicker.

"I mean to find myself a job in Chicago, settle down close by my girl," he says. He glances at Sherry. "I got prospects." When she doesn't say anything, he clears his throat. "I done some security work in the past."

Sherry stares at him, expressionless. "I don't expect Candy knows any of this."

"No ma'am, but I mean to talk to her." When her stare persists, Atwater stands and moves to the edge of the patio. "I ain't looking for handouts." He takes a swig of beer, looking out at the garden. "That Candy always was a nut for the ducks," he says. "She used to collect them." He turns to look at Sherry. "When she was a girl."

"I reckon she still does. You should see the house." Sherry laughs suddenly, and takes another swig of beer. "Damn birds everywhere."

"The house," Atwater repeats. "I could use the bathroom."

"We got one," Sherry says. "No skin off my nose." She gestures to the back door, showing Atwater the flat of her hand.

Atwater moves carefully. Though he doesn't look at her, he can feel Sherry watching him. The heat and the beer are working on him powerfully, but he tries to act the part of a respectable man. Inside the house, it's so dim he has to stop and let his eyes adjust. He finds the powder room just off the main hallway, small as a closet, smelling of lemon and—it shouldn't surprise him, but it does—the nutty, acrid undercurrent of cigarette. Atwater closes himself in and leans against the door. A torn pack of Kools is propped against the window and Atwater helps himself to one, tucking it into his shirt pocket. In an open medicine cabinet, bottles of pills and lotion line up neatly. Atwater pops four aspirin then does his business; when he exits, in a rush, his hip catches a hall table so that framed photos shudder and topple like dominoes.

Cursing, Atwater picks up a dinky framed snapshot of a dog in a Halloween costume—one of those rat-like creatures, hardly a dog at all—and props it back onto its tiny metal leg.

"See the kids?" Sherry says, and he almost knocks the ridiculous dog over again. When had she come in? She shoulders in next to him, grunting slightly and adjusting one of the bigger photos. A wedding portrait. His daughter has aged considerably: her face, scored with lines, has lost the ripe fullness of youth; her hair possesses the flat, frank sheen of store-bought dye. It is long, straight, dark—darker than he remembers. Candy's husband is bigger and older than Atwater imagined, his lush hair peppered white and brushed back from a moon face that's ugly but genial. Not a vain man, Atwater decides.

He looks at his daughter again, his mouth pinched with curiosity. All the women in his life have busted like clocks by the time they were fifty. His mother, worn translucent in the service of others, including himself, had given out at forty-two. His baby sister died years ago, drowning in a quarry lake the first time she ever cut school. And Karenmary: Karenmary was dead with the cancer before her forty-fifth.

"Pretty thing, your girl." Satisfied that Atwater has seen what he should, Sherry takes the portrait back, rubbing the glass with the hem of her shirt before fitting it back in with the others.

Candy isn't, of course, but she looks happy, cheek almost

touching the ruddy cheek of her husband and her eyes caught in some soft, yielding version of relief. Candy has gone on and created her own family; standing in his daughter's decent, ordered house, Atwater decides she'll make it past her forties, and he's happy for her, happy for himself maybe. Because isn't it some comfort that his daughter has turned out all right, despite the lack of him? The single light of the hallway shines like a firmament; when they get back outside Atwater almost swaggers.

"Let's have another beer!" he says, and Sherry, sinking back into her lawn chair, laughs, the hoarse chuckle of a pigeon.

"Sure," she says. "I expect I could be persuaded."

Atwater cracks two more and downs his own steadily, throat working.

"To the kids!" His voice snaps with joy and he dances a little jig, feet shuffling and slapping the patio stones. Sherry laughs with real delight, and he executes an awkward twirl before collapsing into the canvas chair.

"Bravo!" Sherry says, and he holds his bottle to hers. "To the kids," she echoes, and their bottles connect in clumsy toast.

—

Sherry tells him she's a caretaker for the elderly, and that when she gets a good business going, she'll move out on her own. "Bobby—that's my son—he's been good to me. Your girl, too. Bobby's daddy left me with nothing, but that was his way." She shrugs, and Atwater tries to guess whether Bobby's daddy is dead or just gone.

"I have only the one client just yet," Sherry confides. "Miz Grace, over in Earlville. I clean for her, make her meals. Was there just this morning, point of fact. She likes me just fine."

Atwater tips his beer and says that he doesn't doubt it. "You are a woman of many talents," he says. "As I am a man of many talents."

He is hardly slurring his words, and Sherry raises her beer. "You're not so much the piece of work I might have expected," she says. "I gotta admit, you first show up and I think the worst." She leans forward, regarding him shrewdly. "Candy and me, we're close. She's the daughter I never had. So I look out for her."

"And I am glad of it." Atwater pops open another beer and takes a pull. "Candy and your boy," he says. "They look a pair, happy as lovebirds."

"Oh yeah, them two make a nice couple all right. I try to do right by them." Sherry nods vigorously, then casts him a cunning look. "But isn't that always the way? Don't we always try to take care of our own?"

"Oh yeah. Oh yeah." Atwater leans forward. "Does she like her job? Candy?"

"She does okay."

"Does she want for much?"

Sherry gestures around the patio. "As you see."

"Does she talk about me?"

Something flits across Sherry's face, too fast for him to catch. "Well sure she does," she says finally. "You're her daddy."

All right then. Pleased, Atwater lets his eyes sweep the patio. If he lived here he could put a barbecue grill in the corner. All of them eating burgers or chicken, shooting the shit. Even Karenmary would have had to admit that no one could beat him for outdoor cooking. The beer, he can cut that out gradual.

And he could apologize. *I'm sorry that dog hurt you*, he might say to Candy, and mean it. *I coulda stopped the damn thing, daughter. I shoulda had my eyes on you.*

A sudden, unbidden fondness for Belle, a warmth bordering on nostalgia, leaks through Atwater. God bless the woman, after all: she got him here. He looks around, at the patio, the neat siding and yard. To want to be a part of something, that's a different animal from just needing it.

"Lookee here." Grunting, Atwater leans over and unlaces his shoes, then peels off ribbed brown socks. His feet are long, and he wiggles them in the slight breeze that has quickened; he and Sherry are sitting in shadow now. Atwater bends his left leg, arcing it so that he might pick up one of Sherry's empties with the strong grip of toes. "See what this guy here is capable of."

"Bravo again!" Sherry says, her voice husky. She's well on her way to a drunk, too, Atwater guesses. "You're something, all right."

"My right foot's stronger." Atwater looks up. "I believe we have some things in common. Do you see it?"

"A man like you might want to make a little extra cash," Sherry says. Atwater turns to her, but in the purple shadow he can't read her face. She flops her hands and starts to giggle. "I got a job for you, Cy Atwater. We can take my truck."

—

The old woman's house is at the fringe of town, where the lawns have gone loose and ragged, not demonstrating neglect so much as an inability to keep nature at bay. The ditch beside the roadbed is a frenzy of weeds. Atwater cranks his window down to smell the green of it.

"Miz Grace done give me this TV but hell, the woman's too old to help me move it. I could use a man," Sherry says. "Works me like a horse, Miz Grace, but at the end of the day she's all right."

Atwater shrugs. Sure, he can help out. He imagines mentioning this to his daughter, later on, and the pride he might justifiably take: *When I see someone needs help, well I just jump on in.*

Sherry drives her truck with pushy concentration, jerking the wheel so that gravel rattles against the undercarriage. The old woman lives in a gaunt farmhouse at the end of a rutted lane that Sherry takes at high speed, the truck concussing powerfully side to side, jolts like hot wire laid along Atwater's spine. It is a relief to reach the house, which has a derelict look, its gutters hanging at crazy angles, but someone has tucked geraniums into the weedy planters and laid the flagstone path up to the front door. Grass and something thick-stemmed have tilted the path stones here and there, so that Sherry stumbles and Atwater must jump to catch her arm.

"Thanks," she says, and then fumbles a key from her shorts pocket, fitting it to the front lock.

In the door: a pane of glass, set at eye level, divided into diamonds of red and gold. It glows like agate when they step inside the house. "Look," he says, pointing to the burning colors, but Sherry has moved deeper into the dim hallway.

"It'll be in here," she says, and nods through an archway. In fact he can hear the television now, a blur of canned laughter and static. Some sort of game show.

"Damn thing's on." Atwater squints in the dusky light. "Whyn't we turn on the lights?"

"She must've left the set going. To keep away the riffraff."

Sherry laughs. "Now you just stay where you are. I'll wheel it on out." She steps through the archway and the television noise stops abruptly. There is the metal shriek of wheels and the sound of a cart, bumping. "Hell! Cart won't get through the door."

Atwater steps to the archway. The cart with its huge, awkward television, Sherry leaned up behind it, blocks his entry. He tries to peer around her into the dark room but Sherry snaps her fingers. "Cy! Pay attention, man. We got to move this thing."

The living room, Atwater decides: he can just make out a piano behind Sherry, its cover drawn, and a blank spot where the television probably sat. Opposite, in the nearest corner and obscured by the wall, must be a chair, for he can see the ottoman, on which a pair of feet rest, shoeless, the toes misshapen in their cast of nylon hose.

"Hey!" he says, pushing against the cart. The nylons are of the same pale, thick, and shiny material his own grandmam used to wear. The feet are plump, the ankles swollen from their labors. "Howdy, ma'am!" He turns to Sherry. "I thought you said she wouldn't be home."

Not looking at him, Sherry pushes back against the cart. "Help me, Cy."

"Hey!" Atwater says again.

"She's sleeping, Cy," Sherry says. "Leave her be." She leans into the cart. "Let's get going here."

But Atwater gives another shove, pushing the cart into the flesh of Sherry's hip so that he can squeeze through. "Cy!" she cries, but he ignores her.

"Ma'am," he begins. "Mighty kind of—" And then, "Christ Almighty!" The woman's snub nose and high cheekbones are a faint, hard blue in a porcelain face; even in the dimness he can see this. Atwater backpedals, meaning to reach for the reassuring plush of Sherry's upper arm, but catching air instead. Outside there is a commotion of birds. "Holy God, she's dead!" For he had seen the old woman's eyes: surprised, perhaps gratified, covered with a film that trapped the light.

Sherry, watching him, sighs after a moment. "Okay. I meant to tell you," she says, then shrugs. "She's been dead only since this morning. Went natural-like, watching her stories." She cricks her back, leaning first to the left, then to the right. "Don't go giving me that eye," she adds. "I'll call her children. She promised me the TV. I wanted to spare you the details."

Atwater sniffs the air. He feels a current of dread, starting low, rising steadily to his throat.

"I just don't want to deal with the daughter," Sherry says. She draws out one cigarette, then another. She lights both with a clear plastic lighter and holds one to him. "The daughter. She's a bitch, that one."

Atwater squeezes roughly past and into the hallway, blood beating behind his eyes. When he gets to the door he presses his forehead against the stained-glass panel. The world outside, the dry lawn and the sky like a bowl, is red and then gold, distorted by the wavy glass.

"Our kids deserve a new set, you know?" Sherry continues, her voice confiding. "They ain't got but the portable. The reception's shot to hell!"

"I'm done with all that," Atwater pleads. He thinks of Candy's house, all those birds as decoration, like a child might do.

"Miz Grace is dead," Sherry says. "She ain't gonna be missing no TV."

"The daughter will, then."

Sherry, still sucking on her cigarette, joins him in the hallway. "We'll leave Miz Grace her *TV Guide*, okay?"

Atwater recognizes the look she casts at him: flirtatious, eyes creased in what could pass for merriment.

"We should call the police," he says weakly, turning back to the door, to the future he'd imagined for him and Candy, captured in the bleeding, bright diamonds of glass.

"Listen!" Sherry grabs Atwater's shoulders, turning him to face her. "Listen here. I took good care of Miz Grace." She shakes him, back and forth, not exactly rough. "Her daughter never gave her the time of day. That girl was a bitch, if I haven't mentioned it."

———

The bar, Northern Lights, has timbered walls. There are mossy deer heads and fish mounted, shiny and gaping, in their coats of shellac.

"What kind of music do you like, Cy?" Sherry returns from the jukebox, broad hips shimmying. She carries two highball glasses in one hand, like a waitress.

"Skynyrd. No. Miles Davis." He tells himself that Sherry would not listen to jazz. She thrusts the glass into his hand and studies him, lips pursed.

For a moment Atwater hopes it's fear flicking in her eyes, but then he sees the mockery.

"A person's got to take care of herself, right, Cy?"

"Right." Picturing the TV in the back of Sherry's truck, Atwater stares at his hands. It was heavy, the television, its guts concealed in a protruding plastic shell that set off the balance and made it hard to carry; the two of them had to wrestle it to the truck bed. They had worked well together, as it turned out, crab-walking across the dead woman's flagstones, the television slung between them, digging into the joints of their fingers and bowing their backs. On Atwater's narrow palms is a lifetime's accumulation of calluses, ridged and yellow as coins.

"It could have been different," Atwater says.

Sherry's broad slice of a mouth is open a little. "Cheer up," she says, sliding a battered twenty across the sticky table. "Cash for a job well done." She studies his face, then laughs and digs in her pocket again. "Ten more if you'll keep your mouth shut. We don't want to disappoint the kids, right?"

Atwater stares at the money. He won't be seeing his daughter, he could have told Sherry then; he doesn't want Candy's house to be the place where his true nature will blossom, again and again.

"Take the money!" Sherry urges, jutting the round nub of her chin at him. "It's yours! That old woman was done with this world." She winks at him, a specious, sodden wink that seems to take effort. "Folks like you and me, we ain't half done yet!"

"That's the truth," Atwater mutters, sorrowing. The cash under his fingers is rough and warm.

In the weeks and months after the picnic, Atwater would wake sweating from a dream in which he was the one to grab his daughter and hold fast. Always he and Candy had cleared the dog's jaws.

In the scenario he has imagined dozens—no, hundreds—of times, so many times that it is as well worn as memory, he works his will.

He revises. If there hadn't been time to get clear of the dog after all, at least he could have folded Candy close. With his own broad hands he would have covered his daughter's eyes, protecting her from what lay ahead; he would have been the one to scream her name, and when the dog came on Holy God so be it: they would meet what came next together, and so in some way be spared.

Nature

The doctor called them phantom limb pains, the electric shocks that woke her most nights, leaving her gasping and clutching above the elbow where there was still something left to grab. Sometimes her husband would wake too, fitting himself against her back and wrapping his long arms around her, tight, but when Preach slept hard and deep it was just her alone, and the feeling that her hand was still there, poor little rabbit torn in metal teeth.

When morning finally licked under the blinds like gray water, she'd lift her arm and laugh joylessly, knowing that there was nothing left to hurt, nothing but dead air, her arm ending bald and smooth just below the elbow. It was a relief when the doctor prescribed a full run of sleeping pills. He wrote in his crampy hand and told her that these pains weren't uncommon, they were just the brain, catching up. She's still taking the pills, just in case.

She washes the limb daily, with a thin scum of soap and warm water. The male nurse showed her how. He's called Gofer, like a character on TV, and Nikki likes and trusts him. She's learned how to take good care of what's left of her arm, thanks to him: knows enough to rinse tenderly and thoroughly and pat dry with a towel. Right after her limb healed she had to toughen it up as part of her occupational therapy, her OT. She would sit in front of the TV with Preach and, wincing, dip the limb into a Tupperware container of uncooked rice that she held in her lap. Dip and swirl: she hated this, but it did the trick. She wears her prosthesis—a twist of aircraft metal and tough polymer, snugged against the stump—without much pain now, usually all day long.

Nikki also has a prosthetic hand that is useless, but pretty in a waxy way. Most days she wears the hook. It is blue-gray aluminum, with two canted fingers, and operates by a harness and cables, and the way Nikki moves her shoulders. Made of Dacron webbing one inch in width, the harness crisscrosses her back, the straps connected securely with a metal ring. Nikki can put it on herself in the mornings—like shrugging into a coat—and she wears it over an old T-shirt of Preach's that keeps her skin from rubbing ugly-red and sore.

The rest of her appearance has gone to hell. She hasn't gotten a haircut since the accident, and she'll wear her flannel nightgown, the white one that's silvered sheer at the elbows, all day if Preach doesn't have the energy to ride her about it. This morning, though, he comes to sit beside her on the sofa. The TV isn't on yet, but she's hitched up her nightgown, which holds and releases the smell of her like sour breath, and surrounded herself with a stack of magazines. None of the articles in any of them is longer than a page.

"Why don't you work in the garden today, baby?" Preach says, his hands on his knees. He's a tall man, handsome enough, with thick-nailed hands and hair so dark it looks dyed. "Go see. It's pretty; a little wild, but pretty."

Nikki used to love the honest effort her garden demanded, but that was before her car sailed off the highway and into a ridge packed so hard it was like running into a cement wall. She remembers riding the thermals silently for a sun-spangled moment, like the goshawks at her parents' place, but then the car split open with a singular burp of metal. When she got back from the hospital, Nikki abandoned her garden the same way she's abandoned her life—with a bitter, dead-eyed thoroughness. The gardening book she bought the first year they had the house is stuffed on top of the fridge, with the needlework she can't do anymore and an empty fishbowl lacquered with dust.

Preach leans back into the sofa, like he's not going anywhere, and Nikki stiffens. She knows what he's trying to do.

"Go see," he urges again, and in his voice she can just discern an exaggerated patience. "It needs you."

He pats her knee, not her arm, and Nikki knows he thinks he's being sensitive. What she thinks is that he's afraid of it, the assemblage of metal and plastic that acts like an arm but doesn't look like one. At night, he has fallen into the pattern of joining her in bed only after she has removed her prosthesis, laid it on the floor, and turned off the bedside lamp. He will hug her in the dark, face buried in her neck, but his hands never stray; Nikki and Preach haven't made love since before the accident.

"Call me at work and tell me about the garden," he says, and finally stands, picking up his cap.

Preach won't be home from the garage until late. Nikki saw his calendar: the oil changes and tune-ups set back to back, well past seven. As he walks to the door, she allows herself the confusing luxury of pitying him. His days are long, and lately the soap he uses has betrayed him: a rash saddles his jaw with angry red flecks.

Preach pauses, his hand on the doorknob. "Do something," he insists, turning toward her, but gazing over and past her right shoulder.

"Don't patronize me. I know I'm no good to anyone like this," Nikki says in a hard, little voice. She means it, but a part of her also says this to get him to look at her, which Preach does, and which Nikki regrets as soon as she sees his eyes.

"Anything, for God's sake," Preach continues. "It's been— how long? You haven't gone anywhere but the doctor's since the accident. I know where you're coming from, Nik—I *do*, don't look at me that way. But Jesus. You've got to pick yourself up and, and *move on*. That's right," he says, almost to himself. "Move on. Life is passing you by, baby." He plucks at the bill of his cap, warming to his argument. "We don't get more than we can handle in life, that's all I'm saying, okay?"

"Bye," she says in her ugliest voice, lifting her good arm dismissively. When Preach slams the door, the day stretches out before her, flat and sere.

For an hour or more she sits exactly as he left her, poised on the couch in an attitude of waiting, her stomach uneasy with caffeine. The sun has risen like a blazing egg. If she were a different person, she'd be strong, but Nikki misses her hand, the slender, callused fingers; she misses the scab, colored and sized like a beaten penny, left from when she tried to help Preach with the car. Before the accident she had been reckless and exuberant, just twenty-five years old yet sure of her place on this Earth. Now she cannot imagine how to reclaim that world in all its hale possibility.

Nikki uses the remote to turn on the TV. It's still weird to be home this time of day; before the accident, she worked as an assistant manager at the local Ace Hardware, and most days she left the house when Preach did. She liked the job, and the discounts she got on things for the house, but after her disability runs out she's not going back. The kids she supervises are barely out of high school, and Nikki doesn't think she could handle that lethal mix of adolescent indifference and scorn.

And yet it seems that her grace period has run out, or almost: Nikki knows that Preach and Gofer are in league to get her thinking about what she wants to do next. Just last week, Gofer gave her some bullshit brochure about "Prosthetics and Your Career," and when she joked that hardware stores weren't exactly a career, were they, Preach had said, "Well it's a *start*," not seeing the humor in the situation, even though those two were always telling her to lighten up. *Fuck*, she thinks. *Fuck*.

She flops back on the couch, but she's bored, and restless; at 11:30 she gets up and wanders into the kitchen. A stack of dishes leans in the sink, streaked with food and smelling some. Preach knows full well she's been learning to handle dishes at OT; he did them himself after the accident, but he must be on strike now, six months later. It's been almost four days and there aren't any clean dishes left. Nikki knows this because she had to fill a cardboard bowl, meant for dip and left over from a party in her previous life, with cereal this morning. She stares at the stacked plates, then out the kitchen window. The day has taken on a brassy glare, sun bouncing off the white-painted garage so that it hurts to look. Next to the garage, in a wedge of shade, scrawny phlox gasp, gawky and miserable in the heat.

"Damn," Nikki says. And then, thinking of the look in

Preach's eyes, "Okay, okay." She steps out through the breezeway and heat smacks the top of her head. Crab grass thrusts up between the stones of the path Preach laid out last year, and round, thieving violets have moved into the spaces between the lilies. *Nature is messy*, Nikki thinks, *brutish*. And yet, if she is between lives, the garden is not: it continues to uncoil with a slow, sinuous greening. Nikki respects that. She fills the plastic watering can, steadying it with her prosthetic arm, and waters the phlox first. She makes sure the ground is dark and saturated before moving on her knees over to the bed of lilies; with her good hand she seizes a fistful of violets, pulling the delicate stems together into a bouquet. They yield easily enough, clots of earth clinging to their pale roots. A bee drifts down, fat as a Buddha, and Nikki grabs another handful of violets and tugs.

It turns out to be easy, tucking her prosthetic arm against her chest so that the leather hinges at her elbow are flexed to the limit. Giddy, she moves toward the fence separating their property from the next-door neighbor's. She has never met the man, who moved in about a month ago and whose name she cannot recall. Preach has, though. "Nice enough," he'd said the day he met the guy and reported back to her. "But God*damn* he's big."

Nikki's surprised at her progress: she's almost up against the fence now, a litter of naked and uprooted violets fanned out in a wake behind her. She'll have to remember to come back with a bucket. Standing, she notices what Preach probably wanted her to see all along: he's planted a row of chalk-colored impatiens. Their flat, white petals are melted like frosting from the heat, and the leaves, usually so broad and glossy, are folded, embarrassed-looking. Nikki tilts the watering can and watches, mesmerized, as silver water fans down.

"Looks good," someone says, and Nikki can't help herself, she screams. On the other side of the fence is a man with the largest head she has ever seen. He wears a cap, and a hank of thin, dark-brown hair pasted to his brow; his full face is cratered like a moon above a shirt made of plaid-scorched twill. "Whoa," the man says, and his voice is friendly but shy, like a dog afraid of getting a smack. "Didn't mean to scare you like that."

He extends his hand over the fence and Nikki sees he's wearing canvas gardening gloves as wide and brown as loaves of bread.

"Feldon," he says. "Feldon Breen."

She remembers to offer her left hand to shake, and the man clasps it, his eyes on her face.

"You're our new neighbor," Nikki says. He's younger than she imagined him to be—probably in his early thirties, like Preach—and Nikki is suddenly aware that she's in her nightgown, that her hair is oily and uncombed. "I was just going in to clean myself up."

"You have a beautiful garden. You'll have to give me some pointers." The man nods and turns to leave. From the back, he reminds Nikki of a mountain, immense and sloping. The sweat that darkens his shirt fans up and out like a tree.

"Yeah, no problem. Name's Nikki." As soon as the words are out of her mouth, she wishes she could take them back.

Feldon doesn't turn around but raises his hand in salute.

———

"I met Feldon," Nikki tells Preach when he comes in the door. It felt good to be outside today, and she's close to admitting it; she wants to put forth the garden as a peace offering. She's even combed her hair, pulled it away from her face in an effort to please him.

"The big guy, huh?" Preach looks tired, his face creased and dirty from the shop. He clutches a sack of takeout chicken in one hand and a six-pack in the other. "Hey, I got us dinner."

They eat right from the bag, not talking. Preach has brought to the table a sports magazine he must have snagged from work; he peers at it, worrying the edge with his thumbnail, and fails to mention her hair.

Look at me! Nikki wants to cry, but instead lays into her chicken with a grim determination. There is gristle in the meat, and yellow threads of fat.

"Do you think I'm pretty?" she blurts out.

Preach looks up. "Nikki, why are you asking me this?" *Say yes*, Nikki thinks, but a part of her is already . . . what? Defeated? She has never been a beauty—her face is narrow as a carrot, her hair an unremarkable brown—but until the accident, she never felt at a distinct disadvantage.

"Nikki, you are always beautiful to me," Preach says. He sets the magazine down deliberately.

"Right. Go back to reading," she says flatly. "I can tell you want to."

"Nikki . . ."

"I mean, God forbid we should have a *conversation*."

"Jesus, I—"

"I'm serious. Go back to your article."

After dinner Preach takes his second beer to the porch and sits looking out at the garden. His face is so shadowed in the porch's yellow glare that she retreats, past the stack of dishes, to the living room, where she clings to her yarn afghan, drawing her knees up tight to her chest.

—

The next day, Nikki waits until Preach is gone before she turns off the television and opens her gardening book. She is reading about ground cover when the doorbell buzzes, two shorts and a long.

"Feldon," Nikki says when she opens the door, for there he is, a green stalk in his hand. It's stifling outside. His wide, white face is shiny, and Nikki thinks of the protective oil that coats the scales of a fish.

"I thought you could tell me what this is," Feldon says, handing her the stalk with its hollow stem and ragged, pointy leaves.

She smiles faintly. "That one's a weed." Nikki stays where she is, leaning against the doorframe, and although she should be embarrassed by the greasy stench of her hair, she isn't. Jesus, he's big as a bus; what does she care what he thinks? Nikki remembers something Preach said once, how their new neighbor never seemed to come outside on weekends.

"Well," she says finally to Feldon. "You like gardening in the middle of the day, when it's hot?"

He eyes her, his smile fading to a dash that becomes lost in the flesh of his face. He shrugs. "No one's out right now. Most people are at work. A big guy like me." His voice trails off; wiping his hands on his pants, he turns to leave.

"You don't work?"

"Used to be a cop. I got hurt."

Nikki tries to imagine him in uniform and is briefly amazed by the thought of so much blue polyester—the sheen of it, stretched to the limit.

"I am in-between jobs myself," Nikki says, oddly formal. "Most people in this neighborhood work, though," she adds, staring at his back, as broad and flat as Texas. Nikki and Preach drove across that state once, before they got married. They stayed in cheap motor lodges and had sex in the flimsy shower stalls; they drank Mountain Dew to stay awake on the long drives. She remembers, four years later, how when you were in the middle of Texas, you couldn't imagine what any other state looked like.

Feldon turns around. "Yeah, what's with these people?"

They smile at each other and Nikki leans forward, spreading her shoulder blades so that the control cable flexes and her hook snicks open. Without hesitation, he takes it in both of his hands. They are a fragile blue-white, mapped with veins that ride close to the surface, and they cover her hook completely, metal subsumed by flesh.

"Pleased to meet you," Nikki says, and she is surprised, warmed even, by the shy gratitude that courses across his face like light on water.

—

At noon of the next day, she stands near her bedroom window and watches Feldon weeding in his garden. He's bending over with what looks like a lot of effort, his face florid, dripping. When Nikki finally goes outside, it's almost one o'clock. She has pulled on a pair of jeans she hasn't worn since the accident, her nightgown stuffed bunchy and soft into the waistband. Preach always said she looked cute in these pants. *Cute.* She walks up to

Feldon, who has abandoned his weeding and now pounds nails into the fence that separates their lots, the hammer looking lost in his fist, like a toy.

"Afternoon," she says, raising her good arm in greeting.

He looks up and says, "Hey," smiling like he means it. "I'm fixing the fence a little. Couple boards loose."

She stands in silence and watches him pound nails. He seems sure of himself, the way Preach looks working on a car, and there's something nice about standing in the heat, the fence rising neater after just a few thocks of Feldon's hammer. Nikki watches a few minutes more, then turns to get her watering can.

"Damn!"

The steady sound of the hammer stops, and Nikki turns back to see Feldon hopping from one foot to the other, hand tucked into his armpit and the hammer thrown down. He's surprisingly graceful, and Nikki notices for the first time his tiny feet.

"I missed," Feldon says, and she can't help it; something about the look on his face makes her laugh, and then he does, too.

"Let me see," she says, moving to the fence and reaching over. She pulls his hand close and sees the nail split and the flesh around it turning puffy and blue. "Can you move it?" He wiggles the thumb obediently, and she lets go. "Not broken," she announces. "You might want to cover it up, though. Got any gauze?"

Feldon cocks his head, and Nikki says, "Oh, just come over. I'll fix you up."

In her pink-and-green bathroom she's clumsy with the gauze, holding it still with the hook and working the scissors to cut a ragged strip with her good hand. Standing close beside her, Feldon has a strong smell, unalloyed by detergent or deodorant.

Nikki cannot help but breathe him in, and it unnerves her, renders her more awkward and slow. But Feldon's face is calm, and when she's done he grins, although his bandaged thumb is probably twice its normal size, wound with a thick pad of gauze and taped with a white stripe of adhesive.

"Thank you," he says, still grinning, and he tips his baseball cap and leaves.

It's not until he's out the door that Nikki realizes what he's wearing under his overalls: an old pajama top, long-sleeved and polka-dotted, the flannel rubbed thin and the red spots bleeding in all the worn places.

—

Most days they begin gardening at one. Nikki helps Feldon with his weeding, because she's seen that the bending over and working close to the ground is hard on him. In return, Feldon does the heavy work in her garden, the pruning and lopping. She won't go with him to Wannemaker's to buy the things they need—mulch and something called DE for the grubs, a new weed digger when Nikki's old one breaks off at the handle—but she writes out the lists, and afterwards, when the day spools down and commuter trains start moving through from downtown, they go into his house for snacks. Feldon lives in a tri-level, a brown-carpeted warren of cramped rooms crisscrossed with stairways. Someone has taken lemon oil to the ugly wood paneling; the rooms are spotless and, with the exception of a glossy conch shell displayed in the TV room, bare of ornamentation. Nikki and Feldon fall into the habit of watching TV together and eating whatever Feldon has on hand: Twinkies, or the zebra-stripe Little

Debbies with their bars of icing. Feldon brings them out on a green-rimmed plate.

"We're having a party," he'll say, switching on the TV to a game show or one of the after-school specials. The air conditioning is always cranked high, and the blinds drawn against afternoon glare.

"I bought this house with the money I got from my mom," Feldon says once. "That plus the disability."

"What's wrong with you?" Nikki asks. She is eating her Little Debbie slowly, taking nips of the frosting, waiting for the sweet cream to reveal itself.

"I got shot," Feldon says. "When I was a cop in the city." His voice is casual, and Nikki isn't sure that she believes him, but when he pulls up the edge of his flannel shirt she can see a lumpy scar, swollen and rusty against the masses of flesh that lap over his ribs. "The doc says if I hadn't been such a big guy I would have died."

Feldon lets his shirt drop and Nikki nods solemnly. He is sitting next to her on the couch, close enough to touch, and she realizes that she wants to put her arms around him, the whole one and the other one, and reach as far as she can, like holding the world.

Instead she leans over and picks up the conch shell, pressing it to her ear. "I can't hear anything," she says, and Feldon moves his head close—big and square, like an elephant's—so that Nikki's hand, holding the shell, jerks involuntarily.

"You can't hear the ocean?" he says. "Sad." He touches the metal of her hook, once, with thick fingers.

She waits for a moment before saying, "I was driving," in a small voice, and then she sets the shell down. They are both very still. All around them, the clean house creaks. "We had a big car, like a boat, no air bags. Can you believe it?" Her voice cracks, trying for a laugh. "I swerved to miss a pileup, went right over the guardrail. Jesus. Jesus." She hasn't told anyone this, not even Preach, not in this way. "You know, there's a sound that bone makes. I could hear it."

Beyond the blinds, Nikki knows, the hot, crazy world is moving like a rocket. "Goodbye hand," she says.

"Well," Feldon says. "What a fucked-up thing to happen to someone like you."

And it must be the sugar, but her blood is humming: she hears a roaring like a shell should make, a red-and-white noise that fills her ears and calms her, the way Feldon fills her eyes right now, the way Feldon fills that spare, cool room. Nikki stands abruptly.

Later that day, she is relieved to have left when she did; Nikki knows how close she came to something she couldn't take back.

———

The days unreel, humid and gold-capped; the sky gleams brassy blue, as if it has been polished. Nikki wakes these mornings and feels a pleasant, comfortable sensation all along her spine and the backs of her legs; she is loose-jointed and happy in the knowledge that she'll be working soon in the garden, alongside Feldon— close to the earth and its shouting green.

"Preach sure works a lot, doesn't he?" Feldon observes one afternoon. It is past four, and Nikki is curled on his couch, her hair moving in a shaft of air from the AC unit. Another time he says, "If I were Preach, I wouldn't want to be away from you so much."

Nikki fixes her eyes on the television and flushes happily when he voices these things. "Oh, he tries to be there for me," she finally says, so as not to appear disloyal.

A week passes in this manner, and another; the first Wednesday of August dawns gray but clear, and Nikki pads outside early. She's prepared to lazily weed until Feldon appears, but when she makes her way to the phlox behind the garage, she stops short. She's ignored this part of the garden for more than two weeks, and in that time a thick white fur, spotty and ugly, has appeared on the leaves of several plants.

"God!" Her lip curled with distaste, Nikki strips off a handful of the mottled leaves. She thinks about calling Preach. They've been getting along better: she's helping with the dishes—even putting some thought into cooking again—and perhaps as a result of this, Preach hasn't mentioned a job in weeks. There's some sort of truce going on, Nikki figures, although its terms are unclear. They still haven't had sex.

Nikki stares at the disfigured leaves in her hand now and, after a moment's hesitation, goes to Feldon's door. When he answers her knock he is so solid and comforting, so broad and plaid in his long-sleeved shirt, that she feels better. She allows him to drive her to Wannemaker's, where a ham-faced college kid tells her that her phlox have powdery mildew, common enough.

"Your other flowers won't catch it." He stares at her hook before pointing her to the aisle of fungicides. "It won't kill them, you know. Ugly as hell, but it won't kill them."

Nikki feels brave until she hits the aisle, which is crowded with shoppers and their flat, wheeled carts. She stops, the hook thrust behind her, but then Feldon steps up and tucks her damaged arm into his with authority. Together they find the fungicide, and

Nikki buys it; she clutches it in her good hand on the ride home.

"Thank you," she says, once in the parking lot and again when they pull into his drive. She leans over and touches his broad, white cheek. "It's been a long time since I've been out in the world." Feldon looks straight ahead, but she can see a flush creeping steadily up his neck. Outside the car, cicadas roar.

"You know, there's this festival," Feldon finally says. He swallows audibly. "Close by. If we go together, I won't care if people stare. At me, I mean."

Nikki thinks about Feldon's bulk, how it filled the aisle at Wannemaker's. "Yes," she says firmly. "I want to go with you." Something is stirring low in her belly: slow and familiar, it feels suspiciously like lust. When Nikki turns to Feldon and smiles, she likes the dazzled look he wears, and the way the tree beside their car shivers, delicious, in the pitiless August heat. Nikki opens the car door with difficulty. "Okay," she says, hand on the door; she makes herself think of Preach and the life they share. "See you later." She presses the car door shut with her hip, bends her head low to catch him smiling at her. "Goodbye," she mouths through the glass. Nikki hugs the fungicide. She calculates how long it will be until she can see him again.

———

"You're getting fat," Preach says teasingly one night when he gets home, and it's true, her khaki pants are stretched tight across her butt and she's got a little belly. "If you don't watch out, you'll start looking like that cop next door!"

Nikki, who figures it's the Twinkies she's been eating, reaches for him, snapping her hook. "Shut up!" she jokes. "I feel good!"

She can laugh because she doesn't care about the extra weight, or what Preach thinks of her thickening hips.

He's been laughing, too, feinting and ducking away from her playfully, but now he sits and his face grows wistful. "You know I'll miss you," he says suddenly. Preach is going to his brother Teddy's house in the south of the state for a couple of nights. Teddy just bought an old Camaro, and Preach has promised to take a look at it. The car needs engine work, and Teddy will pay Preach for his trouble.

"Are you sure you don't want to come?" he says.

"Nah, I gotta work on my garden. I'll be fine." Nikki turns her face away. She hasn't told Preach that she'll spend one of the nights he's downstate going to the carnival three towns over with Feldon. No reason why he shouldn't want her to go: Feldon is their neighbor, for Chrissakes, and Preach would probably be delighted she's finally going anywhere. But when she thinks about the festival, she feels excited enough to fear how her voice will sound if she tells Preach. "I'm gonna miss you," Nikki lies, and in a rush of guilt, she puts her good arm around her husband and squeezes tight.

—

She prepares herself carefully and waits like a stranger in her own living room. The dress with its three-quarter sleeves is new. Nikki ordered it from a catalog, and the effortless cotton, floating with flowers, makes her feel light. She's replaced the hook with her prosthetic hand. In its skin of flesh-colored rubber, she decides, it almost looks real.

Right at five, Feldon rings the bell, two shorts and a long. He has used the sidewalk, not the gap in the hedge like he usually does, and he waits sweating on the porch in a white shirt made of stiff fabric like sailcloth, and chinos that strain mightily at the waist. On his small feet are dress shoes, leather-soled and pointy, polished like good apples.

"M' lady," he says, bowing low and then holding out his hands to both of hers. "You look gorgeous."

Struck dumb, she accepts his arm and teeters across the lawn on stacked summer heels.

They drive in Feldon's old Chrysler, and in what is meant to be an exuberant gesture, they leave the windows open and push their seats back. But Nikki remains quiet, subdued, and Feldon fiddles with the lighter on the dash as he drives.

"Where's Preach?" he finally asks, and Nikki is angry with herself for feeling guilty.

She starts to reply, but then her hair flies around in the breeze, sticking against the wet of her lips, and she laughs. "He's not here," she finally says, still laughing.

Feldon looks over. "Apparently not." Relief is bright in his face, and something eases between them.

Parking is available on a side street lined with small frame houses, and from there they walk to the festival. It covers three blocks of a main street marked off with sawhorses. The women they pass are dressed for the weather in strappy Ts and shorts, rubber flip-flops spanking the pavement. People sit on the curb, eating gyros that drip with sauce and torn meat, and some of them stare, but instead of a burning awkwardness, Nikki feels special. She glances at herself, reflected in the plate glass of storefronts, and in that swimming, distorted image she looks small and feminine next to Feldon, her hand unremarkable—and beautiful for this. Feldon buys them corn dogs, and shaved, flavored ice that towers high in paper cones. He nods at the wooden tables set up under a tent, but Nikki shakes her head vehemently: she wants to walk in the shimmering evening.

"Look!" Feldon says. "Look!" He points at a black dog with a bandana around its neck, which darts across the street, chased by a woman with a huge polyester ass.

"Yes!" Nikki laughs; she understands that it has been a long time since either of them has been somewhere like this. Lemon ice drips down her chin and she wipes it with her sleeve. It is so humid that her hair is frizzing into a giddy, unmanageable tangle, but she doesn't care. Tonight, she is beautiful: perfect and whole under a sky so violet that her heart expands, aching in her chest. Overhead, a string of lights colored blue and orange comes to life with a buzz.

She and Feldon stop where the game booths begin, the Shoot-the-Bear and Whack-a-Mole. Kids in tank tops clamor for a chance to win the big prizes, which are cheap and huge: stuffed red dogs and crappy-looking tigers with matted fur.

"I've always wanted to do that," Nikki says. But she's looking beyond the games, to an open tent where a woman sits at a card table, chin on her fist. A cardboard hand cutout, taped to the edge of the table, declares in bold lettering: *Your Fortune $5.*

"Looks like a ripoff," Feldon says, but he follows her to the tent. The woman straightens in her chair when they approach. She's younger than Nikki, with clear, coffee-colored skin and a spill of dark hair partly concealed by a square of blue chiffon.

"I'd like to know my fortune," Nikki says.

"Five dollars." The woman points to the sign. "Cards or hand?"

"Pardon?"

"I can read your cards or your palm. Customer gets to choose." The woman looks past Nikki to the stream of passersby. "Faker!" a kid in a concert T-shirt yells, swaggering by, and the fortune-teller gives him the finger. She turns her gaze to Nikki. "Cards or palm. Money up-front."

Nikki digs a five out of her purse and sits down on the little folding chair.

"Hand," she says, and places her prosthetic, palm side up, on the table.

She looks up at Feldon, grinning. He opens his mouth to say something but then doesn't, his face puckered with worry.

"Okay," the woman says. She has to notice that Nikki's hand is plastic but she doesn't say anything, just pulls it close and glances at it briefly. "You have a soul mate," the woman drones. "You're about to start a business. You'll have three children." She steals a glance at Nikki. "You will meet great adversity but you will overcome it. Okay," she says, and pushes Nikki's hand away.

Nikki laughs and stands. "Let's go," she says to Feldon.

They walk about a block before Feldon mutters, "God, that was stupid."

"No," Nikki says. "I got a fortune. Just like everyone else here." She gestures at the crowd surging past. The string of lights, hissing over their heads, colors Feldon's face so that it seems lit from within: for a moment, the neon throb of the fair seems to go still, pulling away like the tide.

"Do you believe what she said about a soul mate?" he asks. Nikki dips her chin in what is almost a nod. "Life is so Goddamned lonely, isn't it?" Feldon says, and his hand closes on her false one. He pulls it to his chest.

Nikki imagines that she can feel the damp material of his shirt, the slick, hard press of the buttons. "Feldon," she says. He grips the false hand and stares at her nakedly; mustard has dried in a crust at the corner of his mouth. Nikki thinks that if she were to lay her head against his chest now, it would yield. But she doesn't do this, nor does she pull her hand away.

"Do you think we get what we deserve?" Feldon asks. "Life is so random. I mean, how do the bad things—how do you deal with what you get?"

The music from the carousel behind him surges back, so loud and tinny that Nikki can barely hear him. When she looks over his shoulder, she can see wooden horses whirling violently past; it's hard to imagine why the children riding their glossy backs are smiling. Nikki steers his hand to her mouth and kisses it gently. His knuckles, beneath her lips, are as white and smooth as a child's. "I'm tired," she says. "I need to get home, okay?"

Feldon guides her through the crowd, his hand near the small of her back without touching it. It's full dark now, the sky unfurled into purples and blacks—except to the east, where the horizon bleeds a dull orange: city light. The kids have gone home, and couples have started congregating under the beer garden tent near the live music. They lean into one another, laughing, passing plastic cups of beer back and forth to be sipped. In the space of an hour, the fair has grown up into something tougher, sexier; by the time they get to the car Nikki's trembling.

"Do you want AC?" Feldon asks, and when she nods he leans over and switches the air conditioning on, his arm brushing her leg.

Too close for comfort, Preach would probably have said, and thinking of this—thinking of her husband—Nikki smiles painfully and looks out the window at the neat houses they pass. All the messy lives going on behind those clean, paned windows. *Good luck*, she thinks, and hugs herself so that the cotton of her dress sighs against itself.

When they pull into Feldon's driveway, Nikki leans over and kisses him, fast, then slips out her side of the car before either of them has to decide what happens next. "Good night!" she calls, her cheeks burning. From inside her own house, she waits for his porch light to wink on, then goes to the kitchen to splash water on her face. There she finds a procession of ants marching across the kitchen floor, and a message waiting for her on the answering machine: Preach, his worried voice queerly distorted by the recording so that it sounds as if he weeps.

Things aren't going well with his brother's car, and Preach is staying downstate a few days longer. When Nikki calls him back, his voice is muddy with disappointment and loneliness.

"Nik, where were you? I tried you a couple of times on your cell, and at home, too. You never picked up."

Nikki smoothes the skirt of her dress and looks out the kitchen window at Feldon's house. It was an accident, she tells herself, that she left her cell phone at home.

"I went to that summer fair we read about. Remember? Our neighbor—you know, Feldon?—he said he'd drive me." The blinds are up at Feldon's, and she can see the blue-white fizz of the TV, an eye of light in the darkened living room. Nikki wonders if there's an unfamiliar lilt to her voice, or if she's talking too fast. "It was okay," she says. "You know: games, rides, bad food."

"Feldon? The fat guy?"

Nikki stiffens. "Our neighbor. Feldon," she repeats.

"Huh," Preach says, and they fall silent, breathing at each other over the phone.

"So," Nikki says brightly. "What's going on with the car?" Over in Feldon's living room, a broad shadow crosses the TV screen, briefly blocking it. Feldon, getting a snack. Nikki looks down at the line of ants and wonders how they'd like Twinkies, the rich, animal-fat cream. She imagines herself eating a Twinkie, sitting on Feldon's couch.

"—and I thought you could come down here."

"Huh? Preach, I'm sorry. I missed that." Nikki turns away from the window. "What did you say?"

"I said I'm waiting for some parts and I'll be here through Friday. I'd like you to come down, Nik. I miss you. What are you doing up there, all alone?"

"Oh, I've got tons to do." Her voice trails, then heats with sudden inspiration. "The garden! The garden would go to hell."

Preach is silent, and Nikki imagines his face, stubborn and disappointed. He's probably standing in his brother's kitchen, leaning against the wall with the vegetable-pattern wallpaper.

"The garden," he says finally.

"Aw, honey, don't be disappointed. You'll be back on Friday and we'll talk every night between now and then." Nikki turns to look out the window again. "I'll make you a dinner," she says absently. "Listen, we'll have a little party, okay?"

Preach says nothing.

"Okay?" Nikki repeats.

"Yeah, sure." They are quiet for what seems like a long time.

"Well, God," Nikki finally says. "Here I am, getting back into the swing of things. I'm taking care of the garden like I used to: better, even. I would think you'd be happy."

"Yeah, it's great that you're into the garden now. Terrific." Preach's voice is tight, coppery with hurt. "But Jesus, it's not like you're looking for a job or anything. Yeah," he says hotly. "A job. I'm working my ass off down here to keep you in, in—fucking *tulip* bulbs, okay? When are you gonna get over this thing with your arm and get a job, for Christ's sake?"

"A job?" Nikki's voice is low, incredulous and angry. "You just don't get it, do you?" She closes her eyes to conjure Feldon's face. "Is that all I am to you, some *pay*check you're missing?" Her voice rises; she's thinking about her old gig at Ace. No way would she have time for gardening with Feldon if she took another job. With the sharp edge of her heel, Nikki grinds part of the ant procession into paste. "Like you understand anything about what's left of me!" Nikki drops her good hand, the one holding the phone, and searches the window for a glimpse of Feldon. When she brings the phone back up she can hear Preach sucking in his breath. Before he can say anything, she slams the phone into its cradle, realizing, with something like amazement, that she doesn't know Feldon's phone number.

She heads over, still wearing her good dress. He has changed into pajamas and greets her as though there were nothing unusual about her showing up at a quarter to ten, and they watch an old Montgomery Clift movie and share a tub of pistachio ice cream.

"He was in a car accident, too, you know. He became deformed," Nikki says of Clift. She and Feldon are pressed close on the couch, eating right out of the carton, spoons clicking, the thin cardboard of the container leaving a wet corona on the fabric of her dress.

Nikki's not sure how many movies begin and end before she finally goes home, but she does know she falls asleep for a while:

when she wakes, the TV is off, and the cracks between the blinds show the blank, grayish-green of a new day. She pulls the blanket close around Feldon when she gets up; his nakedness makes her quake.

Back in her bedroom, Nikki removes her crumpled dress and stands before the mirror, staring at the contours of her heavy breasts and thinking about the sweetness in Feldon's face. He smiled when she stroked his scar, tracing its rough topography with the curved fingers of the false hand. She doesn't care that Preach has left three text messages. What she cares about is the tender way Feldon undressed her, granting the same sober attention to removing her prosthetic arm as he had to slipping her dress away.

———

Nikki waits until noon to call Preach back, and when she does she keeps one eye on the clock; she'll soon be gardening with Feldon.

"Will you still make me dinner when I get home?" Preach asks, and Nikki says, *yes, of course,* anything to get off the phone, for Feldon is leaning on the fence in his canvas gloves and cap, looking over at her window. As soon as she hangs up she's sorry. Preach probably envisions some sort of romantic make-up dinner: handholding and candles, that bottle of wine Teddy gave them last Christmas. Jesus. She walks outside, shaking her head, but when she sees Feldon, gnawing on an apple, she gets an idea.

"Hey, how 'bout dinner on Friday?" she asks him when she reaches the fence. His face is open and flushing, and Nikki is suddenly loath to tell him that Preach will be there, too.

She almost says it that night, as he fumbles with her buttons in

front of the TV, but they are too eager, too hungry; when she
starts to speak he puts his finger against her lips. "You're my
queen," he murmurs. Later, she watches the blue light of the
television move in waves across their naked flesh, and she decides
that the dinner is inevitable and—and what? Feldon's eyes are
closed, and Nikki lets her good hand play across his belly,
remembering how his hands cupped her breasts, sending a
thrumming down into the channels of her legs. She imagines him
declaring his love for her: over meatloaf, mashed potatoes, and
the frozen corn soufflé that's hard to find in the suburbs now.
There is a confused image of Preach standing up and challenging
Feldon, then retreating, but she does not dwell on this; most
particularly she does not dwell on her husband's unhappy face.
Feldon is so much clearer in her mind. When will he welcome her
to life inside his house? A week from now? A month? Nikki
strokes Feldon's closed eyelids, which are a transparent plum in
the watery light, and gazes past them to the prosthetic arm. It lies
where it fell, tangled in her clothes, and she shakes her head. She
has never been the kind of woman to attract more than one man
at a time.

—

Nikki knows how to clean a toilet one-handed. On Friday, she
pushes the vacuum cleaner with her hook, and hauls out a
tablecloth, along with candles shaped like ears of corn that she
thinks look funny and festive.

"Okay!" Nikki says. She gazes at the clock over the sink, a
pressed-plastic owl she and Preach got as a wedding gift. Nikki
stares at the ugly tan plastic and understands that the digital

readout is positioned somewhere in the owl's nether regions, something she has missed before. The owl's *colon*, she thinks with distaste, then realizes that she can't remember whether Preach said he would be home at two or three. But he arrives closer to four, the rash on his jaw more pronounced: a spattering of red like angry seeds. He hugs her awkwardly.

"Nice spread," he says when he notices Nikki's table. She's put out the candles but not the plates. "Corn. Cute."

He sets his small blue suitcase down and pushes his hands through his hair. "I missed you," he says, and Nikki nods, unwilling to match the urgency in his voice. "It wasn't the same without you; I don't know if it was good, being apart for so long."

"Preach, it was a week," Nikki says evenly.

"Well. But it's been way too long since you and me . . . well, you know. Don't you think?" His voice is almost embarrassed, and he reaches for her, grabbing the fold of flesh that has started to lap over her waistband. "More of you to love these days."

He's trying to be funny, Nikki knows, but there's desperation in his thin face and she turns away. Feldon's bulk: it has heft, and rhythm. Each night this week he has slipped into her and moved above her with something like grace. Preach's hand is heavy and without eloquence, a boy's grab. She turns back to her husband, and sees that his eyes are dark with fear. *Let the best man win*, Nikki thinks coolly, but what she says is, "You unpack," and then gently removes his hand from her waist. "There's beer when you're done."

Which he helps himself to, after he has carried his suitcase upstairs and pulled on a clean shirt. They sit facing each other in the living room, sucking cold, yellow-tasting beer out of cans in a walleyed silence under which resentment quivers like gel.

Feldon comes to the door at precisely 5:15. They both jump to their feet when he rings, and Preach's voice is a little too loud when he opens the door: "Hey. Hello. What a surprise!"

Feldon, pink-faced in a cotton turtleneck that pleats tight across his chest, clutches a box of candy wrapped in foil, a stuffed dog secured to the lid. He steps into the house and the two men stand gaping at each other. When Feldon holds out the candy, Preach takes it, bewildered. He looks at Nikki with a mix of astonishment and hurt, but his face is nothing compared to Feldon's, which is a mask of pure anguish.

"Preach. Feldon. You've met, right? I thought tonight would be a great time for us all to get to know one another better!" To no one in particular, she says, "You need a beer," and when she gets to the kitchen she leans against the refrigerator, closing her eyes. She can hear Preach in the other room, his voice strained but polite, and then Feldon says something back. It takes Nikki a while to tear the top off the bag of chips, to get a beer open and into a glass. By the time she comes back into the living room, carefully gripping a tray with her good hand and the hook, both men are sitting.

"Reggie Jackson," Preach is saying. His face has a shiny, tight look that Nikki recognizes: he is warming to his subject. "Nineteen seventy-seven World Series, Game 6. Three swings, three home runs. Best World Series moment I ever saw. Looked awesome, even on TV." He sits back with a satisfied look.

"Kirk Gibson," Feldon responds immediately. "Nineteen eighty-eight, Game 1." He shifts in his seat, apparently gaining confidence from the fact that he has Preach's attention. "The guy limps up to the plate to pinch hit with two outs, and he knocks the Athletics out with one swing. Reggie was great, but Gibson's home run was more in the clutch."

Preach hoots and the men grin at each other, then look surprised to be grinning.

"Treats!" Nikki sings.

Preach studies his hands and Feldon takes his beer off the tray without looking up. "How about Willie Stargell's home run in Game 7 of the '79 Series?" he says.

So, not the queen tonight. "You're welcome." Nikki feels a crackling of irritation, like sparks. Jesus Christ Almighty: as if Feldon is even *interested* in baseball. "Chips!" she says, then sets the tray aggressively down and remains standing, unsure whether she should join Feldon on the couch or pull up a dining room chair. She's pretty sure she set her beer down somewhere. She casts her eyes around the room, finally going back to the kitchen to fetch a new can. When she returns, Feldon has his hand in the bowl of chips and a rapt expression on his face.

"Chryslers? Pretty damn good vehicles," Preach says. "You get what you pay for, you know?"

Feldon laughs, a craven gurgle Nikki instinctively hates.

For the next twenty minutes, Nikki moves back and forth between living room and kitchen. Her face is hot and bright; she's rushing to get the food out, yet can't imagine what she'll do when there's nothing left to serve. The men don't look at her, but they eat the chips and most of the dip, then get started on a tray of crackers and sausage that Nikki sets out. She's just returning with a glass bowl of peanuts when she hears Preach say, "Yeah, I'm lucky I've found something I really like doing for a living. Can't complain about the garage; they do all right by me. Now if we could just get Nikki back to work. She needs to get out more; I think she's still pretty freaked out by her hand."

As she steps into the living room, Feldon says in a hushed voice, "At some point she's just going to have to accept her—her *situation*, you know? I'm sure it's hard for her to see that right now, but a job . . . yeah, a job would be a good first step."

Feldon's voice trails off when he looks up and sees her; she's caught him nodding vigorously, basking in her husband's attention. Preach looks up, too, and Nikki squeezes her eyes shut. She thinks of the phlox, the fat purple blossoms disfigured, irreparably, by collars of furred leaves. She slams down the bowl of peanuts and faces Feldon.

"You're fat," Nikki says. "You could do something about it, but you don't."

"Jesus!" Preach grips his beer and stares at her.

Feldon pauses with a loaded cracker halfway to his mouth, and Nikki can see the split in his nail where the hammer hit, its blue-and-red language. He lays the cracker down almost delicately on the edge of the tray. His face is inscrutable. "Yes," Feldon says. "I am that."

"Eat like a pig, look like one," Nikki says. Her voice shakes. "What I mean to say is, you get what you deserve."

When Feldon stands, Preach moves to stand also, knocking his beer to the floor, where it fizzes gently into the carpet.

"If you'll pardon me, I think I may have to take a rain check on dinner," Feldon says.

Even in her agitation, Nikki can see that he addresses Preach, not her. "Listen to me!" Nikki begins in a loud, panicky voice. The men are standing next to each other, shoulders almost touching. "I don't deserve this!" she cries. Nikki holds her prosthetic arm out, shaking it at them so that it rattles. "I deserve to be . . . whole!"

Then Preach is stepping forward, putting his arm around her in a proprietary way. "Feldon, Jesus, I'm sorry; she's not herself." Feldon turns away from them, pulling at the collar of his sweater. Through the windows the day pours yellow, and Nikki knows how hot it is out there, the sun tireless and bright, glaring down on the impatiens and the lilies and the poor, benighted phlox.

—

She and Preach make love that night, urgent and frantic so that it hurts, really; afterwards she lets him hold her while she cries.

Since that night she has tried to define in very clear terms what she has lost: an arm, not her life, she tells herself sternly, again and again. And each time she remembers to be grateful for this, just as she is grateful that her husband is a decent man, capable of forgiveness. In four months they will have their first child. She'll be a competent, loving mother, she thinks, and she has decided that the most important lesson she has to teach her unborn child—Nikki is convinced it will be a girl—is that you've got to learn to be alone. *Another person can't make you whole,* she counsels her unborn daughter. *So you'd better learn to love the depths of your own heart.*

But still.

Some nights, despite the cold, she'll go stand on the front steps, where she can just barely make out the lunar light of the television in the cracks between Feldon's blinds. Snow covers the dead stalks and branches in her garden, but she can still remember the living room, the plush sofa; the humid, lingering taste of pistachio ice cream. Feldon's hair parted on the left. His back extended flat and wide.

But what she thinks about most is his scar. The skin around it was as pink and brave as the inside of her elbow, that tender spot just above where the false arm has to begin.

Six Foot

"You're crying, Mama," Anna says, solemnly handing Jools her ragged stuffed owl.

"Oh, not really," Jools sobs. "Silly Mama." She climbs into the tub and takes the child into her lap, pulling the shower curtain to. *Children adapt*, Jools decides. She sneaks a look at the round of Anna's cheek, which is softly furred, like a peach, and about the same color; her daughter's eyes and pocket of mouth are calm. "We're hiding," Jools says, feigning a giggle, and then Anna laughs, too, so it's all right then, isn't it? Not too scary for a child of five. She makes believe that the two of them are in a boat, the child's weight against her knees a relief, a comfort and assurance that she, Jools, cannot float away.

The tub is the color of a pearl, tarnished yellow around the drain. Her mother's tub, from which Jools can still hear the hum of conversation: all those funeral-goers downstairs. Nance, her sister, is down there somewhere, and it's Nance who finally comes to get them, barging right into the bathroom and smelling the way she does, of apple shampoo. At least she doesn't pull the curtain back.

"Reception line," Nance orders when Jools peeks out, trilling "Helloooooooo" to make her daughter laugh, to distract Anna from the way Nance shakes her head with its tilting crest of hair. There was that whole business at the funeral home, of course; a little scene, really, and Jools should be ashamed. But she is fed up with Nance, the way her sister doesn't like her, not much, and the way Nance bosses everyone, even Mr. Anders, the funeral director, with his liver-spotted face and proper dark suit.

It's true: lines were crossed. Jools had hissed during the wake, "Dad liked me better." Or maybe she'd said that he liked her best, but it was only in retaliation. Hadn't Nance said, loud enough for Jools to hear just before the service began, and to an old Mason friend of her father's, the bluff and red-faced Bill-somebody: "Well, she's here as you see; dressed to the nines, isn't she?" Meaning her, of course. Jools. She didn't own a pair of pumps and so had worn ballet slippers with her dress. Black ones, for God's sake; it wasn't that she wasn't taking care. Their father was dead! And yet the two of them could not seem to get past the petty grievances that had dogged them all the long years since their childhood, even now, even today obsessing about who got the consolation of an approving hug from ancient Aunt Eleanor, or who seemed to hog the limelight at their own father's funeral.

Did Nance hear? Oh, certainly: the way she stiffened her back and hinged forward on her hips. Jools tells herself she would have apologized, set things right, but for the flurry of guests: Eleanor, to whom Nance had been ministering, and all the obese second cousins. It was so confusing: their father had only been sixty-eight when his heart failed him, when his lungs filled with water and he died. They'd only had thirty-one years together, Jools thought; it wasn't fair. Nor was it fair that Nance, older by ten years, had had more time. Maybe *that's* why she'd said it, Jools thinks, wrapping her legs around her daughter; they might have been tobogganing, welded together in some spurious, joyful descent.

"You need to be downstairs. Now," her sister says. Nance thinks Jools is sentimental, immature; nothing like Jools sees herself, which is to say: funky, funny, smart. Kind.

And so the reception line must be gotten through, with the attendant agitation about who might stand where. As it turns out, a perceptive neighbor man settles it, someone who might have witnessed the trouble between them at the funeral home: Jools on one end, Nance on the other, and their mother, bewildered and supported by the starchy Eleanor, somewhere in the middle. This is the way it's done, he insists when Nance argues. Jools keeps Anna beside her, understanding that all the years she has lived have been a prelude to loss. *All the years we have to make ready*, she thinks. But nothing prepares you for extended absence. Nothing readies you for the permanence of it, the terror.

Jools feels Anna grip her hand. There are so many unfamiliar people here, kissing with their grieving, pursed mouths. Jools looks over at her mother, whose eyes are wide and red, glossy as cinnamon candies. At the funeral home, Mom had pulled her aside; she'd pressed a check into her hand and implored her to be patient with her sister. "I've told Nance the same thing, dear," she'd whispered. "You two have got to start getting along." The check was one Jools' father had written out not one week before; money is tight for Jools, everyone knows it. He'd signed it in blue pen, his sturdy backhand signature comforting her when she folded the check in her wallet, even as it made her cry.

—

The funeral ended, finally, and the day after that. Jools agonizes about whether she should call Nance. What if they don't ever talk again, after all? But another day passes, and then a week, and the thought of picking up the phone sets her, fingers twitching, to cleaning. One morning she scrubs the bathroom floor, digging at the grouted tiles with a toothbrush. She is both astonished and frightened when her sister calls on *her*, almost two weeks to the day after the funeral. *Calls, comes calling.* That's how Jools thinks of it. Anna is off painting unicorns at kindergarten, either that or gluing glitter to her jumper, and Jools has the day off. She is a waitress at a diner, the kind that serves breakfast all day on place mats laminated with strange yellowing pictures of food; the idea was that she would write, too—poetry, mostly—but it turns out she underestimated how exhausted she can be at the end of a shift and so she hasn't been writing, and certainly not since Dad's heart attack. When Nance arrives, late in the morning, she leans on the bell until Jools buzzes her in.

"Shouldn't you be at work?" Jools asks, standing just inside her apartment door, arms braced across her chest, as her sister strides down the carpeted hallway in a cloud of fruity perfume. Nance is a secretary for a local builder, or maybe she's the office manager. Shouldn't Jools know which? Has she really not been listening? "Anna's not here," she says. If it were just Jools here, in this apartment, Nance probably wouldn't ever come at all.

"I know, genius, she's at school. I've come to see *you*; I want you to see this house," Nance says. For a moment, silent recriminations dart between them. Nance has hinted that she disapproves of Jools' current arrangement, which for almost four years has been the waitressing plus a healthy subsidy from their parents. "It's not easy to be a single mom," Jools explained to Nance once, though she doesn't miss the father, a drunk who might be dead. Anna's never met him. Jools doesn't remember exactly what Nance said in return, but she knows the spirit of it, something about no one's life being easy.

"So you'd better get dressed," Nance says. Today she's wearing office clothing: dull kitten heels, a skirt. Too much makeup, but still. Nance has always been the pretty one. Jools' robe is whimsically patterned with moons and stars; over the left hip is a darker patch of cloth where the pocket has torn away, and her short hair is dyed, vivid as cherry cola, to cover the gray. Never reserved, her temperament tending to loud, sometimes messy enthusiasms, Jools does not trouble to hide the fact now that she has been crying. She is a person who bleeds outside the lines, possessing a happy, seedy energy that draws people to her, even as, she suspects, it allows them to feel superior.

But today she is so tired, and though it is only 10 o'clock she is too weary to pretend—what? Pleasure at Nance's visit? Vigor? Optimism? She has to save her energy, in any case, for when Anna comes home from school and needs to see her mother happy. "No," she says reflexively; what does she care for Nance's house? "I'm staying in today."

"I have to show you this house and we need to talk. About Mom."

"I'm busy," Jools says, registering the subtle tightening around Nance's jaw.

"Think about someone besides yourself for a change." Nance looks pointedly at her sister's wet cheeks.

"Whatever," Jools says, fingering the sash of her robe. There is a stain there, dime-sized and red. But Jools hates ketchup, and tomato soup; she can't imagine where it might have come from.

"Oh for God's sake, there's money in it for you. Okay?" Nance takes a step forward and braces her hands against the edges of the doorsill, so that for a moment Jools is reminded of a game the two of them used to play as girls. Captain's Brace, they called it: press your arms against the inside of a doorframe for a full minute; step outside and your arms float skyward, unbidden.

"Come in," Jools says impulsively, knowing as she says it that Nance won't. It's the place where Jools is always reading and scratching away at her poems, something Nance, with her hard, orderly way of doing things, can't respect. In Jools' apartment— where Anna has a little bed in the single bedroom, and Jools takes the couch—there is a general, cheerful, slovenly display: stacks of books, even in the bathroom, and school forms and bills and catalogs of things Jools can't afford but loves to look over, jammed in the desk she has painted blue, or weighted under the sugar bowl on the kitchen table. Not dirty: some rabbits of dust, certainly, but mainly just untidy, cluttered. Nance will come sometimes, to pick up Anna for a visit to the zoo, or a movie, but she will never linger.

"No," Nance says, remaining just outside the door.

"Fine," Jools replies. "Fine." It's easier this way—not to argue—easier to go to the house and gawk or admire the cabinetry or whatever Nance is angling for. Who cares about the money? Not Jools. Just get the thing over with, because they'll see each other at Mom and Dad's place, and if she and Nance are fighting, what then?

Mom's place. It's Mom's place, now.

And Jools is lonely. She pulls on shorts and a T-shirt that is almost clean, joining Nance, who waits for her outside in the car with the air conditioning cranked; it's hot for May. Nance drives a big coppery Buick, luxe and regal as a ship, west through what used to be farmland, now carved into subdivisions, and the subdivisions into tidy plots just big enough to contain the raw new homes with their sprawl of bedrooms and baths. Maybe Nance's employer is good at what he does; maybe he can manage to sell these kinds of houses. But just driving by the ugly new construction, Jools feels pity for the families who have to live there.

—

Bill Pepin is Nance's boss, sole owner of Pepin Construction, rich as Croesus. Married. "He's peppy, like his name!" Nance will enthuse about the man in a voice she usually reserves for her two dogs, Mutt and Jeff they're called, ugly shepherd mixes that love no one. Nance and Bill are not having a traditional affair in that they have not had sex—Jools believes this, knowing her sister to possess a rigid honor—but she suspects they've sinned emotionally. Nance has a picture of Pepin, a blurred snapshot from last year's office Christmas party, fixed to her refrigerator with a magnet shaped like a whale. Pepin brought her the magnet when he returned from a trip he made with his wife, off Boston's coast. And Nance is in possession of certain gifts: a dishwasher, a nice-enough cloth coat, and not from Stein Mart, either, that Jools has reason to believe came from Pepin.

"Day off?" Jools says.

"We're almost there," Nance murmurs. They've entered a pretty, hilly area, the farmland dimpling into waves of trees, and there is a creek to cross, blue as cracked ice, and the water fast over stones. Nance cranks the wheel left and the car fishtails down a rutted gravel drive. Second-growth trees lean close on either side, and it's suddenly dark and cool. When they burst into light again, Jools is taken aback: the clearing, neatly mowed, spans acres. In the exact middle kneels a tiny pink house with a slant roof. It could almost be half a house, it's that small, but the siding is immaculate, and there are tomato plants in plastic tubs marching down the front steps.

"We're here," Nance says. She parks and regards Jools for a moment before nodding, satisfied.

"Where?"

Nance makes to open her door, then stops, lips pursed. "Listen," she says. "I need your help." If it cost her to admit this, she wouldn't let on. "This guy. Sunday. I need him to like you."

Nance smoothes her skirt over her thighs, which have thickened, Jools notices. Her own reaction to their father's illness and death has been not to eat, and in spite of her pain she's proud of this, how narrow her own hips look in their ragged shorts. She looks out the window at the little house.

"Pretty back here," she says.

"Yes, and this guy? Howard Sunday? He owns it, all of it. Bill—" Nance stops to let Jools register her secret smile. "Mr. *Pepin*, he wants to buy the land. One hundred acres Sunday owns. We could build back here. The commuters, they don't mind a trek into Chicago when they can get a piece of this."

"I'm not here to shill for Bill Pepin," Jools says.

"You may not have a choice." In the little pink house, a curtain flicks. "Mom can't afford to keep helping you. You've got to make your own way, Jools. You help Bill, you'll get a percentage. Sunday won't sell to me." Nance nods at the house, pink meringue in the flat, greening sun.

When did life become so dreary, Jools wonders. But there is her daughter, she reminds herself, her joy, and for years there were Jools' parents: sensible, loving people born into an era that shaped them into tough, steady adults. Jools' father was with the Pipefitters; Jools' gentle-faced mother raised two children and now these two daughters are all she has, along with the grandchild, Anna. But there is only so much love to go around. And they are so different, Jools and Nance.

"Nothing I can do," Jools says. She doesn't respect Pepin, who wears a hairpiece, frizzed and tangled like kelp. Once, in a fit of malicious fun, Jools had anonymously mailed him a brochure about hair plugs, the pictures glossy and startling.

"Sunday will like you," Nance declares with a shrug. "He likes your type. The artist." She pronounces it "ar-teeest."

"He'll like me or he won't," Jools says.

"I think you can talk him into it," Nance says. "He's taken sick. He can't keep this place up."

Around the house, scarecrows with plastic baby doll heads have been set at regular intervals, their molded faces blasted into indifference by the weather. Only one has hair left, a dark, furious thatch of it laced with leaves and straw. Jools thinks of her daughter, who has come to dolls late, dressing them and murmuring to them after Jools calls Lights Out. There are so many things Jools would like to do for Anna. There are things she would buy her daughter if she could.

"Come in with me. At least meet the guy," Nance says. She's suddenly brisk, the one with the real job who pays her bills early. "He already knows we're here, we might as well make nice."

"He doesn't know we're here."

"He knows," Nance says firmly, and when she steps out of the car, the door to the pink house opens. A man stands in the doorway, leaning on a plastic cane.

Jools stays put, and Nance leans back into the car. "You owe me," she hisses. She doesn't need to say why: Jools knows what she has to make up for. Nance straightens and waves at the man like a prom queen.

"I guess I told you how I feel!" he yells, but Nance moves assuredly, extracting a foil-covered pan from the backseat and smiling her secret smile. *She walks like a man*, Jools thinks, trailing behind her. When Nance's heels sink into the soft earth near the house, she keeps going, her steps broad.

"I want you to meet my sister. She's handy enough," Nance yells, and Jools is to understand that Howard Sunday can't hear. He waits at the door for them, though, and when they stand side by side before him, he squints.

"She ain't your sister," he says.

"She is," Nance insists, "and she baked you this." Nance holds up the pan. "I told her about your collection."

Sunday peers at Jools, a quickening of interest in his cloudy eyes. "You like dogs, hey?"

"I do, sir," Jools says, nodding, for that's true enough, Nance's two brutes excepting. God knows what Nance has in the pan.

"You related to her?" This addressed to Jools, and she nods again.

"Too bad for you," he says, and heaves off his cane. "Come in, I guess. You find your way." He spins in a slow circle and moves into the tiny living room. There is a broad path to his chair, a recliner covered with crinkled green baize, and another, narrower path that leads past the couch and to the kitchen. The rest of the room is thick with figurines: dogs from the looks of them, china and pottery and plastic. Terriers and setters and tiny stuffed Chihuahuas, set flank-to-flank, or noses touching, arranged on boxes or low tables or on the floor. A bookcase against the far wall staggers to the right, its six shelves packed with dogs. Sunday reaches his chair and collapses into it. Jools can see now that half his face is stiff with stroke. He'd obviously once been a big man, but time has sloped his shoulders, diminished the hams of his legs, until there is only the great melon of a head left, with its frozen face and an astonishing dewlap, soft and white and mashed into the pearl-buttoned collar of a shirt that digs like a garrote.

"Don't get many visitors," Sunday says from the depths of his chair. Then, gruffly: "I like the dogs."

"I can see that," Jools says.

"You like my dogs?"

"They're very clean," Jools says, and they are, remarkably so.

———

Nance has brought a coffeecake from Dominick's, and Jools recognizes it as the apple Danish their mother has purchased and served on Sundays for years, although Nance has removed the cellophane and cardboard foundation, jamming the oblong pastry into a square pan. The frosting bucks like waves on an ocean. "My sister is a wonderful cook," Nance lies. She has brought a knife, wrapped in aluminum foil, and napkins patterned with hearts.

"A treat," Sunday says, accepting a slice. His voice is guarded.

"My sister has many talents," Nance says. "She's handy. An artist."

"Been my experience that artists ain't always so handy," Sunday says, not unkindly. "Hold on." He stands with effort, stumping past them and along the path of dogs. "Can you help me?" he asks, but when Nance rises, he nods curtly at Jools. "You," he says. "You help me. Shoes off in here," he instructs, and so she kicks off her sandals and follows him to the bathroom down the hall, prideful at having been chosen.

The bathroom is tiled in pink; like the rest of the house, it possesses a dignified cleanliness, a taking care that reminds Jools of her parents. The shower, with its handicap rail, stands separate, and the tub is filled with water, she thinks at first, in which small, hard berries float, green and slick.

"I got the Ruckus Juice in here," Sunday says, and when Jools stares at him, he laughs. "Gin, girl. Make my own. I expect your sister could use some. You?" He inclines his head to a blue plastic pitcher that hangs from a chain over the tub. "Dip it up. There you go. Look out for the juniper, though." He's talking about the berries. This batch of gin has been steeping two days now, he says, and it's ready enough. Sunday bites into his square of coffeecake, which he brought with him, folded in the pink napkin. "You really make this?"

"No."

He nods. "I thought you'd tell me true. Well, then, I can tell you it tastes like shit."

Jools laughs, kneeling beside the tub and scooping up gin. "You got the moonshine bottles with the *XXX* on them?" she teases.

"Heh! Yeah, sure I do."

They stop in the kitchen for plastic glasses, patterned with roosters and scored with dozens of lines, like the veins on a leg.

Nance, who hurriedly pockets her cell phone when they enter, accepts a glass of clear warm gin with surprise but not displeasure. "Cheers," she says, and the three glasses click together. "To new friends," she adds, smiling blandly. She tosses back her drink, gasps, smiles.

"Hair of the dog," Sunday says, topping her off from the blue pitcher. "So you come all this way to drink my gin?"

Nance laughs falsely. "Mr. Sunday," she says. "You have a dog problem."

"Too many dogs," he agrees, shaking his head. "I got dogs up my ass."

Jools pretends to sip her gin, which is clear and oily, like turpentine, and contemplates the rows of canines. At her feet is a wooden terrier, its ears planed to uneven points; at home, Anna has plastic men that come equipped with binoculars and tiny, sharp swords.

"Jools!" Nance commands. "Look alive! Could you make this man some shelves?"

Jools gazes around the room. "Shelves," she says, thinking of Sunday's pink bathtub. The man belongs to a different, better generation. "You got bricks? Board?" Jools has made shelves for Anna's books out of these things. "I guess I could help you some."

Sunday stands again, and Jools sees the way he shakes and sways. "I got a shed, some things you might use."

"I could stay here," Nance says. She cradles the pitcher in her lap, her rooster cup empty again. "I'll just hold down the fort."

"You do that," Sunday agrees.

—

When Anna lost a beloved stuffed toy, the child had keened, "Oh dear! Oh dear!" like an old woman, and Jools, who traveled seventy-five miles to fetch it from the turnpike McDonald's where Anna had propped it in a molded plastic seat, understood then that she would do anything—anything—to protect her child from loss. In the lean-to shed behind the pink house, she tells Sunday this story: how she hired a babysitter and drove at night to retrieve the animal, an absurd owl with a mortarboard that read *Class of '89.*

"My life has coarsened me," he says agreeably, and in the half-light of the shed his ruined right eye appears to wink. "As it has your sister. You, though—"

"Nance loves Anna. We both love her." This, Jools has sometimes thought, is the one thing they share.

"There you go." Sunday leans forward, regarding her with pale eyes. "You're like her."

"Who?" Jools says. "Nance?"

"No, no." He is impatient, his legs jerking.

Jools is surprised at how eager she is to please him. "Who?" she asks again. "Tell me who I'm like."

"My own sister," Sunday says. "She lived in this house. The dogs are hers." He looks out the door of the shed, past a scarecrow with its sunlit plastic skull, and to the fields, and then the secret woods. Clouds are coming in from the west, massing just behind the screen of trees. "I guess I added some."

"Can I meet her?" Jools yearns, suddenly, to find someone like herself. She's been lonely for so long and she almost says this.

But he is speaking, his voice curiously rusty: "Well, she's six foot."

Jools pictures a tall, frank woman, striding through her days with curiosity and intent. Thick, freckled hands, a placid face. "Tall like you, then," she says.

"Tall? No. Six foot: she's gone, child." The strong, good side of his face quivers, then stills. "*Buried.*"

"I'm sorry," Jools says.

"Yes." Sunday folds his hands, murky eyes floating past her.

"My father died," Jools says. She picks a piece of wood from the sloping pile against the wall, digging at the soft pulp with her chewed-upon nail. "I miss him. My mother's not dead, but I miss her already. Do you understand?" All those dogs, she guesses he might. Her laugh just leaks out of her. "I'm okay," she assures him.

"Well," Sunday says. "It's all the long goodbye, isn't it?" The light is gold in the shed, and for a moment, Jools feels the joy that you wait for, that comes like a bird, rising.

Sunday sighs. "My sister, you know: only so many people can love us." He nods, his ruined face stern.

"Everything except for my daughter is ending," Jools says.

"I hear you. Don't cry."

His honesty is a relief. So many people have said the wrong things these last weeks.

"My sister wants you to sell this place." The words are rushed, barely above a whisper. "She wants me to convince you to sell. I guess you know that."

Sunday is silent. "Well," he finally says. "She's been trying, that one. Do you plan to? Convince me?" He dips his finger into the crumbles of icing left in the napkin he brought to the shed, licking it delicately, his tongue as narrow and pink as a shell.

"No," Jools says.

"You'll still make me those shelves, then."

"If I can." Jools wipes at her cheek. It is not lost on her, the assumption that he will still need them. "They won't be pretty."

"I guess I don't care about that," Sunday says. He crumples the napkin and leaves it on the workbench. "Best get back."

The floor of the lean-to is rough under her bare feet. "Don't tell her I told you," Jools says.

Sunday draws a finger across his lips. A smile passes between them.

———

In the short hallway leading from the back door to the kitchen, the dogs are three-deep on either side; Jools cannot imagine how Sunday navigates this path. But he does, swinging his cane along the cramped space, his progress a ragged success and Jools just behind him. When she steps on the china collie the sound is muffled; in the moment before the pain she can see how it might all play out, clear as soda-lime glass. "God!" she exclaims. The dog's ceramic haunches pop from beneath, skittering across the floor and leaving a tracery of blood.

"I broke him," she says. Were it not for the blood, she might not have told him at all. And because there is the business of Nance, come running, and the ensuing confusion—gauze must be produced, antiseptic in a corroded-looking tube—Jools almost misses the weight of Sunday's disappointment. He never tells her *It's all right it's all right*, the way she might have expected, though he does pat her foot in its awkward wrappings, when they are seated back in the living room, each with a fresh tumbler of gin, and he warns her, "Be careful." He is trying and failing to fit the broken halves of the collie together, and it's funny in an awful way, how the rhythm of his words matches the throbbing in her foot. She thinks about infection. She understands the power he allows her—the power she still has to hurt him.

They leave almost immediately, she and Nance. "Things went okay until you broke the dog," Nance says. They are standing beside the car, Jools favoring her torn foot, Nance stealing a cigarette before the long drive back. There is the curtain, flicking again: what Jools sees ahead for Sunday, should he sell, is hell in a chair; some residence for seniors, one of the expensive, gabled ones, plush enough but no sort of place for the dogs. Nance twists her cigarette beneath her heel. The shoe buckles in the middle. Her sister used to have the figure of a boy, Jools remembers, and a young man's hard, narrow face, those restless, angry eyes. She's smart, Nance is, school smart, but also about how the world works. *That's what Sunday meant*, Jools thinks: *knowledge has made Nance hard when it comes to other people.*

She is afraid to look at her foot, its rusty leak of blood. "I hate mess," she says.

Nance jerks her head dismissively. "Better he should move while the deal is to his advantage."

"He wants to stay," Jools says. In the hot, yellow grass, a child's swimming pool, patterned with smiling whales and partly filled, has been set out for the birds.

"I don't care," Nance says.

Jools looks down at her hands, and one of them is puffy, speckled: some nameless, painless reaction to the stresses of the day. "Have you ever had hives?" she asks her sister, although she doubts it, her faith in Nance's flawless shell, hard as candy, complete.

Nance ignores her. "Mom won't see Christmas."

"What? *What?*"

"Her heart is broken," Nance says, and when she turns, her face has smoothed into something Jools cannot recognize. "She told me she won't see Christmas, and I believe her."

It's starting to rain: a drizzle like mist, misery in it. "We don't know that," Jools says, not wanting to believe that their mother might confide in Nance rather than her.

"I do," Nance says, and climbing into the driver's seat, she waves at the pink house.

—

As she drives, Nance talks about the pasteboard castles, so many of them Bill will plant here, on that rise, or in the wooded area. The road clings to a ridge, high above the property, the expanse to either side breathtakingly evident. "This one house, with a *turret,*" Nance says.

She's kidding, Jools thinks. A house with a turret belongs in England, not here. "And who will move in, the Disney princesses?"

"The trees will have to go, too."

Jools looks out the window. There is river birch here, far below them in spindly clumps, their pale trunks glinting as if jeweled. "He's got all those dogs," she says. "You don't know that I'll do this."

"I already told Bill Pepin it was done." Nance stomps on the accelerator. "The dogs. The dogs. What do you care about his stupid dogs? You can *convince* that old man to sell!"

"Convince him that he's better off alone?" Jools says.

"You are a disappointment," Nance says.

"Selfish bitch."

"Selfish, says who?"

They will never agree, later, who said it first—*Selfish! Selfish!*—though each is privately certain that she only screamed it back, in retaliation. Of course they agree that in their agitation they batted at each other, the heavy Buick bucking and skidding on that narrow dirt road pocked by rain, and they both remember how Jools screamed when the air bags released, and Nance's nose crushed in a spirograph of spraying blood.

The car ends in a ditch, bleeding steam, and they have to scramble out of the culvert on hands and knees. Up above are the splendid trees, soaring like church spires. *Anna*, Jools thinks. When she picks up her daughter at kindergarten, she can always tell how the day has gone, just by the set of her daughter's face, or it might be even more subtle, the swing of a backpack. That's how well she knows her girl.

"Oh dear, oh dear," Jools breathes, and looks up through the canopy of trees, the sky impossibly far away, the birds, circling, like specks of pepper. They are so high above her, Jools can't even hear them calling to one another. It's like watching through glass. Rain pats down. "Nance?" Though she knows her sister struggles in the weeds just behind her, she stops and waits, eyes closed, for Nance's voice: impatient, even dismissive. Only now does Jools understand her need to hear it; there is Anna to think of, after all. How many people will love her daughter, really love her, when Jools is gone? "Nance!" She clambers onto the sharp gravel of the roadside. Dust from the accident, stirred by the rain, rises like flour around her. "We could have died!"

"But we didn't." Nance's face is tight and shiny, red with effort; even Jools can see the relief in it.

"Are you all right? Are you all right?" they ask each other then, when they have both rolled over the top rim of that culvert, chattering like excited birds. Daubing at the blood streaming down her sister's chin, Jools makes promises that she will keep, up to when and after Sunday himself is long gone—to that gabled retirement community, perhaps, or even dead. But all that is in the future, yet. Here at the culvert, the dust rising around them in clouds, the two sisters are giddy, touching each other's faces, solicitous and embarrassed. "You have a story for Anna," Nance says, and indeed it is a fable Jools will tell the child, again and again: the car, the culvert, the sisters, unscathed. How essential love is. Only later will Jools appreciate the secret she keeps from her daughter: how treacherous love is, also, to those outside its fairy ring.

Sailor Lake

W hen she goes to pick up her husband, he is waiting in the recreation room, slack-jawed, silent, his too-big wedding ring threaded on a length of green yarn and tied around his neck. The rec room is mauve and green, with framed Monet posters on the walls and stacks of *Good Housekeeping* magazines splayed on tiny end tables. Construction paper cutouts gambol in planned hilarity on a bulletin board, and a large, hand-lettered sign reads, *Hello! Today is Sunday, August 10.* Wyckham, called Wick, sits in the center of a slippery pink sofa, waiting for her. His skin is as translucent as a shell.

On her daily visits, Bev finds it hard to reconcile this still, hollow-eyed man with the images she has held all her life of crazy people: red-faced maniacs, nattering and spitting behind bars. Wick's face is collapsed, sucked into itself, and he hasn't talked since being committed.

When Bev takes his arm and leads him to the car, he looks happy to see her, but doesn't say anything. She gets him settled into the passenger seat and touches his thin cheek. "We're going camping, Wick, just like we used to do," she says. His hair has been brushed in an unfamiliar way, probably by the day nurse, the fine, colorless strands coaxed straight across his head and slick with water. "You look very nice," she adds, touching his face again gently, then starts up the car.

Wick closes his eyes, ready for sleep.

"We're going to Sailor Lake," Bev says. She drives with a heavy foot, the car roaring. Ahead, the sky is dead and white; bugs smack the windshield at regular intervals, leaving behind a tracery of clear fluid. It has been a rainy summer and the mosquitoes have become a contagion, floating everywhere in clouds. Bev scratches her neck and keeps her eyes on the road. The tidy farms they pass—red-painted barns, wooden bear or duck silhouettes staked neatly in every front garden—remind her of the house she grew up in. Bev sighs. When she'd first proposed this trip, two months ago, her best friend Ruth had said, "Beverly, you don't need this. Wick's fine where he is. You take a trip. I'll watch the house." Ruth is a good woman, a motherly widow who, well into her sixties, persists on dyeing her hair an eye-popping blue-black. She bought Bev's lunch that day as they sat at a little café table, knees touching. "You need some time off."

Time off from what, Bev wanted to know. And besides, once Bev fixed on it, she couldn't shake the idea. The Sailor is two hours away, one of a constellation of little lakes hidden among the bluffs and seesaw hills of the Chequamegon National Forest. She and Wick had traveled there every summer for almost twenty years, first as newlyweds, shy with marriage and the novelty of new teaching jobs, and then, when Linda was born, as a little family. When their daughter was young they would drive there on a

Friday night and not return until Sunday, sandy and damp, ready
for another week. Linda practically lived in her swimsuit then and
Wick—her Wick! He was ruddy and solid, a grill master who
labored over burgers and bared his arms to the sun. It wasn't until
Linda became old enough to hold down a summer job that the
trips were shortened, then delayed, then finally abandoned
altogether.

Bev steals a glance at Wick. He is strapped securely into the
passenger seat, shoulder bones visible through the thin fabric of
his polo shirt. Bev reaches over with her right hand and rubs his
wasted forearm. She thinks about the quick light she is certain she
saw in his eyes when she first mentioned the trip: in June, mid-
month, on one of the carefully orchestrated day trips the doctor
had approved. On that outing, Bev had driven Wick to an old-
fashioned ice cream parlor she had read about; it sounded
cheerful, she thought, as if planning for a child. But when they got
there the tables were grimy and the music too loud; runny mint-
chip cones in hand, they had abandoned the storefront for a
nearby park, Bev matching her step to Wick's shuffling gait. The
heat had been appalling, and Bev, desperate for the outing to be
nice, to be happy or fun—it would be days before they ventured
out again—scrambled for something to talk about, and thought of
the Sailor. She mentioned the lake and there was that brief light in
his eyes; suddenly the heat was not so oppressive, and Bev was
certain of the impact a place beloved from their past would have
on her husband. She imagined whole decades of his life surging
back to him, filling him with speech, and so had made an
appointment with his doctor as soon as she returned home.

"I think this trip would be good for both of us," Bev said to
the doctor, a severe man with a cleft chin and a mouth full of

square, beige-colored teeth. She told him this over the phone and, again, at their meeting. "This is a good place, a happy place."

"My, well yes. Wick is actually doing very well on these outings. A trip might be a good next step for him," the doctor said, his voice cautious.

Bev had left the meeting feeling expansive, her hands in her pockets, twitching with joy. Now she stops at a gas station outside Prentice to fill the tank. Inside the little florescent-lit Quik Mart, Bev loads up on snack foods, imagining Wick's cheeks pinkening, filling out on cakes and salt. Ahead of her in line, a couple in their fifties laugh and argue good-naturedly. The woman is broad-hipped, with a coarse, plain face, but her husband, whose arms bear the mottled blue traces of a Navy tattoo, holds her hand and calls her "dearie." Bev catches herself staring and turns away. She reminds herself that she has her Wick again, and her relief is so intense she is garrulous. "Going to Sailor Lake," she tells the hatchet-faced clerk. "We're camping. I'm cooking again. Sailor Lake, you know." Bev pulls two crisp tens from her purse and places them on the counter. "We're almost there!"

Wick is awake when she returns to the car, his smile as pure as milk. "Hello, dearie," she says, happy enough. He eyes her bag of groceries, and when she pulls out a packet of chocolate-covered raisins, allows her to pour a few into his palm. Bev doesn't start the car right away; they sit quietly and eat, watching the thin line of birch trees planted around the gas station. The leaves flash like coins in the heavy, syrupy light of late afternoon. Only when a car pulls up behind them does Bev make a move to leave. A *V* of geese flies over low, honking, as she pulls out onto the main roadway, and Bev cranes her neck to get a glimpse of their dapper black-and-white markings.

"Like spats," Linda would probably have said. She was a willful, gap-toothed child who grew to be wise enough not to take herself too seriously. She died in a car accident, just thirty-three. Bev sighs and looks over at her husband. His eyes are already closed, the papery lids flickering.

Wick had always been a taciturn man, but when the small car Linda insisted on buying spun out and under the bristling undercarriage of an eighteen-wheeler, he began talking less. At the funeral, he had towered over the other mourners silently, his grief palpable, shimmering. He had already begun to lose weight then; his dark suit hung from him, as did the flesh of his face. "God, I miss her," he had managed to say to Bev the morning of the funeral, his voice so changed, the effort of this statement so great, that he said nothing the rest of the day, or the day after. Bev was left to greet the mourners, to press their hands and make assurances, to urge coffee upon them, or cake.

The Lord started speaking to him a month or two later. Bev was still working then, teaching eighth-grade English in order to forget the way her lost daughter's hair used to smell like summer, and at first she thought her husband was having an affair. She'd heard of such things: adults seeking illicit comfort in the wake of tremendous loss. And in her incredible naiveté she thought this was surely the next-to-worst thing that could happen, after the death of their only child. He was gone most afternoons when she returned from work, and when she finally asked him where he'd been, he had hugged her, a beatific smile on his face. "I've been to church," he said, and the next Monday, after some thought, Bev traveled home from work a different way and stopped at the Catholic church they used to attend when Linda was small. Wick's gleaming Buick was parked in the lot. When she poked her head in the sanctuary her husband was sitting in the front pew, his sloping shoulders draped in a seersucker sport coat Bev hadn't seen in years. When he returned home that night she fixed him a cool drink, shook pretzels into a bowl, and took his hand.

"Wick, tell me what's going on."

"Bevvy, I'm fine. I'm listening to the Lord," he said. He lifted the glass of lemonade Bev had prepared and held it close against his face so that his eye, peering at her magnified through the cobalt glass, looked distorted and bleary. "I see the Lord in everything," he said, moving the glass away and staring at her imperiously.

"What's the Lord telling you?" Bev didn't know what else to say.

"He sings sometimes. He tells me how things were and how they are. He waves to me from the trees."

Wick set the glass down and jerked his head toward the front window, through which a fine elm and two ragged poplars were visible. He looked so gentle and happy and she felt reassured, but in the days to follow Wick did not speak except in hymn to the Lord, and Bev found herself fighting off worry that skated close to panic. He was losing weight, and so when he cleaned his plate, she took to serving that dinner several nights in a row. One week, they ate meat loaf and au gratin potatoes for five nights running, until he left his meal untouched and she knew it was time to try something else. The nights were the worst: this was when she tended to miss Linda most keenly, and Wick's rapt expression left her most lonesome. But she adjusted. She started turning up the TV, and she talked to Ruth, on the phone, or over coffee and a stale cookie, sometimes, in the little coffee bar downtown.

Last December, though, Bev had arrived home in the late

afternoon and found Wick not at church but in bed, a damp cloth folded over his forehead and his arms rigid at his sides. She managed to get out of him that he had a terrible headache, and so she had scared up the codeine she'd started taking for migraines after the accident, and dosed him enough so that he fell asleep. But when she went to check on him after dinner she found him awake, leaning up in bed and trembling.

"Oh Lord, do not rebuke me in Thine anger," her husband had moaned, rocking back and forth, fists pressed tight to his shrunken cheeks. "Be gracious to me, O Lord, for I am pining away."

She didn't know what to do but hold him—stroke his narrow, arcing back and hold him tight.

After that, he had headaches every day. In the week before Christmas—their first Christmas without Linda—Wick woke screaming, clutching at his head and sobbing that the Lord was bitter and vengeful.

Bev called 911. The beefy paramedics had to restrain him— bind him to the stretcher—for he was flailing and screaming so that the cords stood out on his neck, calling her name but mostly calling for Jesus. "Have mercy! Mercy!" Wick shrieked, and the night, swallowing those cries, had a queer black intensity.

The neighbors grouped solemnly around the driveway, reaching out to touch her arm when she passed, but she couldn't recognize any of them in the red strobe of the ambulance light. She had pulled a pair of Wick's wool pants on under her old yellow nightgown, and there was the rough scratch of them against her shins, and she clutched Wick's hand in the ambulance and promised him that God was good.

At the hospital, pinned under the sterile blue lights of the ER,

Wick had twisted and implored, "He will not comfort me," and Bev nodded helplessly, repeating her husband's name in a whisper until the orderlies sedated him and wheeled him away, to the psych ward, as it turned out, with its green-mint walls and stuttering florescence.

In April, Bev gave notice that she would not return to teach in the fall: the thirteen-year-olds exhausted her—what did they know about sorrow?—and she told herself that Wick would be home by September and certainly he'd need her; she couldn't possibly be gone during the day. Wick has remained hospitalized long enough to see the ice glazing the wire over the windows give way to the mellow light of spring. Now the window in his room is filled with a white summer glare that creeps across the walls and illuminates the Xeroxes he taped there early on: smudgy black prints he asked the nurses to copy from the art book Bev brought in on Valentine's Day. Holy pictures, mostly: the Apostles and Mary, frozen in grainy black and white.

—

She and Wick move north, driving past stands of aspen, birch, and spruce, meadows of bold deer. Wick's face is turned to the window, and she glances over again and again, fixing each time on the patch of tender white flesh behind his ear. Blue-veined, almost transparent, it brings her near tears. In fragile channels, his lifeblood flows, rich and secret; Bev imagines her husband's religion flowing there, also, now that he has taken it inside himself. Sublime insights: she is certain that they move quiet with his blood, waiting for interpretation.

They reach Fifield, with its clapboard Historical Society and modest, small-windowed homes, and Bev slows when she sees the restaurant that marks the turn onto 70—the great plaster deer out front, leaping. Bev glances at the restaurant as she wheels the car past. It's called Northwoods today. Used to be something else, but the deer statue is the same—Linda always looked for it as a landmark. The sun emerges briefly from a pad of cloud, lights up the deer's peeling flank, then disappears.

It was chill and wet the night Linda died; she lost control of the car on autumn-slick pavement, a two-lane road probably a lot like this one. The policeman who came and stood just inside the door removed his hat, exposing a head of abundant hair, ridged by the hat's rim. Bev fixed on that improbably lustrous berm of hair as the man told them it wasn't anyone's fault: the car had spun out because it was small and light. But Bev had secretly blamed the truck driver: because he drove the vehicle that peeled her daughter's car open like an orange, and because—faceless— he was easy to hate. She wasn't prepared for the fact that he would attend the wake, wearing an awkwardly knotted tie patterned with horses, grief distorting his features. When he approached her and Wick afterwards, his hand extended hesitantly, she surprised herself by hugging him. But Wick had stared past them both, his face raised so that he gazed at something above their messy, human exchange.

The car roars east now on 70, which bows and curves, and Bev starts looking for her turnoff. She almost misses it: a sharp right on Sailor Lake Road. She's going so fast that the big car fishtails a little in the gravel, but then she steadies, tiny rocks pinging against the undercarriage. Wick stirs and sighs. On either side of the road, daisies lift their broad, flat faces. Here is Sailor Creek, running through the blooms like gray glass; here are light-hungry saplings, leaning into the road. They brush the roof of the car when Bev turns into the camp entrance. The campground is just as she remembers it: the little sites, each with fire ring and log bench, uneven clumps of birch and maple separating one from another. Domed tents bloom like preternatural flowers, and one shiny old camper, humpbacked like a snail, is festooned with colored owl lanterns. Bev smiles and slows the car to a crawl.

"Look, Wick. Lanterns!" Wick turns to her, as if startled, then follows her pointing finger to gaze at the cheery camper. "Owls. Who would have thought of such a thing?" she cries. "Owls, by golly!" Wick sits forward and considers the lanterns, yellow plastic under a lowering sky. Bev thinks she sees him smile.

They find a site by the lake, which glints a glorious silver between the trees. Bev parks to one side and moves hurriedly around the car to open Wick's door. He is sitting perfectly still, seat belt still on, head cocked in an attitude of listening. Her hand on the edge of the car door, Bev pauses, too. Somewhere on the lake, fishermen are calling to one another, and beneath that sound is the steady plash of the lake on stones.

"We made it, dearie," she finally says, helping him out of the car, pulling a green plastic windbreaker around his shoulders. "Sailor Lake, just like we said." Wick pushes his arms through the jacket sleeves with a look of concentration, then fixes her with a grin of such incredible sweetness and triumph that she is, for a moment, breathless. "All right, then," Bev says. "Okay."

In the past, Wick has always set up the tent, but this time Bev does it, after settling him on a bench by the water with a plaid comforter so that he can watch the fishermen and the fading day. She likes the feel of the aluminum tent poles in her hands, and the way the blue canvas snaps when she shakes it out. But it takes longer than she thought it would to set the poles right and stretch the canvas tight over them. By the time she is done, the day has turned colorless and chill and, her face and hands peppered with mosquito bites, she is possessed by a weary despair. Unpacking the food hamper, building a fire, and cooking are suddenly unthinkable. She goes to gather Wick. Bev sees him before he sees her, sitting exactly as she left him, his long white fingers folded carefully in his lap. Two sparrows peck in the dust by his feet, unafraid, and because Bev can imagine them, fat and cheeky, nesting in his hair, she claps her hands to make them fly off. Wick turns the slightest bit at the sound; when she comes to stand beside him, he offers her a battered smile.

"I thought we'd eat out," she says, her voice loud and falsely cheerful. Wick's face assumes a look of concentration. "We'll eat out, dearie," Bev says. She steps behind him and folds her arms around his thin chest, propping her chin on his shoulder. Together, they look out at the lake. The sun is sinking, burnt-orange, so that the gray waves are tipped red. Against this molten water the silhouettes of two water birds placidly bob—loons, judging from the graceful curve of the necks.

"Ahhhhh," Wick whispers, and Bev waits, not breathing, until it is clear he isn't going to say more.

"Let's go," she says, straightening up and adjusting the blanket on Wick's shoulders with infinite tenderness. "Let's go now."

Wick stands slowly, still looking at the lake, his hands loose at his sides, unsure and spidery.

They drive to Minocqua for dinner, because Bev remembers the restaurants there, family establishments where two people can get pancakes and coffee at eight at night. That's what she craves now, something thick and warm for her stomach. As soon as

Wick settles in the car, still gripping the plaid comforter, he closes his eyes. The Buick thrums east on 70 and Bev, glancing in the rearview mirror at the last bloody blur of the sun, switches her high beams on. This evening is as fragile as glass. She begins to hum, then sing in her scratchy contralto, what she thinks must be a hymn, remembering the unspeakably hot July day she dug out her girlhood Bible. The thin pages were like onionskin, rimmed in gold, and when she flipped through them they gave off an ancient, sweetish odor, not unpleasant. For almost an hour she scanned the pages, looking for clues to the private place Wick now inhabits with his God. It remains her quiet certainty that when she understands this ecstatic place, she will be able to communicate with him, fully. When she finally closed the Bible that day, she placed it on her nightstand, where it remains; she has taken to reading verses at random before going to sleep. One in particular, in Exodus, strikes her so that she marks it. It is about seeing the face of God.

—

When they reach Minocqua, with its gaudy main drag, the traffic surges and slows, past the Pizza Hut, a Kentucky Fried Chicken, a gift store with an Indian theme. She pulls into the first restaurant she can remember from years ago—the scrolled, orange neon of the sign winks at her, beckoning—and Wick sits up, disoriented with sleep, when she bumps over the curb. They walk across the parking lot together and toward the restaurant's bright windows, which look like the lights of a ship.

Inside, the noise of the place comforts. When the waitress leads them to a two-top, handing them plastic-covered menus,

Bev studies the faded color photos of burgers and pie with something like joy. She orders chicken-fried steak and whipped potatoes for them both, then leans back the better to enjoy the clamor and the way the waitresses hustle. She smiles at Wick, who gazes around the hot, brown room, a bemused expression on his face. Two children careen past their table, shrieking happily. Bev laughs. "Wick! I remember coming here with Linda. Remember? Remember?" Wick looks back peaceably. "Linda always ordered a cheeseburger," Bev says. "Yes, that was it. She loved coming here. They knew us by name."

Later, Bev will wonder if she even had the right restaurant, though at the time, talking to Wick, it seemed right, good at least to talk about their daughter.

When their plates come, she lifts forkfuls of steaming fried meat and chews lustily. She is ravenous. For the first time in months, her food has savor. "Look at that baby there." Bev points at the table next to theirs. "No older than Linda was when we brought her camping the first time. What do you think?" Wick, who has dipped his head over his own plate and set to his food without prompting, turns and regards the family at the table next to theirs, where the baby won't eat, throwing Cheerios and little bits of chicken to the floor. He looks back at Bev, smiling uncertainly. "Uh-huh," she says encouragingly. His eyes flicker, but then the baby tips her little head back and screams. Wick grips his fork tighter. At the next table, the father pushes back his chair and in a smooth motion lifts the child from her highchair. He is a dough-faced man, gaudy spots of sunburn branding his cheeks and forehead, and his T-shirt strains across an ample belly, but his eyes are kind and he holds the baby with tender competence. She quiets immediately. Wick squeezes his eyes shut.

"You doing all right, sir?" The waitress has returned with a plastic pitcher of water.

Bev leans forward and says through her food, "We're just fine, thank you; that's all."

Wick looks at her, then at the waitress; he gestures and opens his mouth as if he's going to say something, but manages only to wave his hand vaguely. A triangle of meat dangles from his fork, and Bev can see half-chewed food, wetly obscene in his open mouth. Somewhere a plate falls, the two children run by again, laughing, and Wick lays his fork down carefully; he places his hands over his ears and begins weeping soundlessly. A high color has stained his cheeks—he looks feverish—and he does not respond to Bev, not when she reaches for him across the table, nor when she gets up to stand beside him.

The waitress fumbles for the check and thrusts it at Bev. "Can I get you anything else?" Her face, though concerned, is also curious, and as rosy and unlined as a baby's. Bev hates her for this.

"That's all," Bev says, almost breathless. She manages to smile at the young woman and pays with a twenty-dollar bill, leaving the change. "We're going, dearie," she says to Wick, hooking his arms into his jacket even as he remains, weeping, in his chair. "Can you stand?" Bending, she links an arm around his waist and pulls.

"Can I help?" The young father from the next table is rising from his seat again, his face creased with compassion over his daughter's downy crown, but Bev shakes her head and helps Wick up, disentangling his jacket from the chair, snagging her purse haphazardly around her neck. When she steers Wick out of the restaurant, her arm is bound through his, and they move slowly across the parking lot, leaning on each other, windbreakers snapping. Wick's jaw trembles. When they finally reach the car, she unlocks the door with her left hand and gently maneuvers her husband into the passenger seat. He moves stiffly, a man in pain, and he will not meet her eyes. "Let's go," Bev says, but when she puts the car into gear, she pulls out abruptly, almost colliding with the back of a station wagon parked nearby. Bev slams on the brake and Wick lurches forward in the seat. "Okay, okay now. We're okay, Wick."

In the weak light from the dash his face is green. He stares into his lap. "Wick, talk to me," she says, her voice low. A couple in matching jogging outfits has paused to stare into their car. The woman, who is about Bev's age, running to fat, with crested white hair and a patrician nose, locks eyes with Bev, then grabs her husband's arm and moves on. Bev reaches over and strokes Wick's wrist, surprised at how her own hand trembles. "Wick. Please." Her husband stares back at her, the skin around his eyes tight with panic. His mouth works.

Bev waits, then abruptly starts the car again. Beside her, Wick doesn't close his eyes, even when they leave Minocqua's cheap glare and enter the full dark. Although Bev has the high beams on, it's difficult to make out the road ahead; balsam and pine press close on either side. She feels chill, and when she reaches across to turn on the heat, Wick makes a startled sound, like a moan. The moon revolves across the sky.

"Linda was a happy baby," Bev finally says. They are halfway back to camp, and though Wick continues to stare straight ahead, he reaches forward and braces his hands against the dash. A mosquito has managed to get into the car and it zippers the air near her left ear. She swats at it and the car jumps. "I think so. I know so," she says, wrenching the wheel to the right and stealing a glance at her husband. "Babies cry, you know. You can't take it personally." Even to herself, her voice sounds afraid.

When they reach the campground, Wick gets out of the car before it is fully stopped, and walks unsteadily to the little tent, where he pulls off his jacket and sweatshirt, and lies down on top of his sleeping bag, shoes still on, his face closed.

"Okay, now," Bev says. She pulls the little blister packet of sleeping pills out of her purse and Wick dutifully takes two, washing them down with bottled water. She sits beside him in the tent then, smoothing his hair back mechanically until he closes his eyes and sleeps. When she finally eases herself down beside him, her body aches as if it has been broken.

—

Hours later, she wakes to a rattling sound, followed by the bright crash of metal on metal. She jerks up into the close, black-earth smell of the tent: the sound is jarringly near, but when she reaches for Wick, he sleeps on.

"Wick! Wick!" She keeps her voice low. Outside the tent, the crashes diminish, then grow again, in a kind of rhythm. Her hands cold, Bev worms out of her sleeping bag and grabs Wick's gray sweatshirt, which smells of tobacco, pulling it over her nightgown. She gropes for her glasses and clutches them to her breast before crawling awkwardly onto the smooth ground outside the tent. To her right, the crashes resound, followed by the trill of breaking glass.

Bev presses the glasses on so that the trees—dark, moving shapes—spring into focus. They form a tunnel through which the lake is visible as a lighter gray patch. The commotion comes from the campsite just north of theirs: the metal sound, banging again, and a sort of grunting exhalation.

"Hello. Hello there." Bev steps forward hesitantly, suddenly aware that she isn't wearing shoes. Through an uneven line of new-growth maples, she can just make out the cleared perimeter of the deserted site. She steps closer, and can see something black moving in a blur between the trees.

"Who's there?"

Bev whirls around at the sound of Wick's voice. It is rusty and bleary. He is unfolding his body from the tent, holding their darkened lantern in one hand. When he lights it, with a great deal of fumbling, she can see the shocking boniness of his face, illumined from below, and a circle of tall grass bleached lemon in the light. With the lamp lit, everything outside its yellow circumference is ink.

"Who's out there?"

Bev allows Wick to move past her, through the grass and into the line of trees, holding the lantern high. His step is tentative and halting, and the lamp swings in his hand crazily, back and forth so that light spills across packed earth, a blackened fire ring, an overturned can of trash. Behind the trash can sways a young bear with a gaunt, arrow-shaped head; when the light flies past, the bear rears on its hind legs so that it is about Wick's height. Bev can see its broken claws, ragged and the color of horn.

"Fie!" Wick cries. "Fie!"

The glare from the lantern catches in the creature's eyes so that they gleam gold and then brown like flawed marbles. The animal's fur is matted and patchy, looking in the unreliable light as wooly as a lamb's.

Bev gives a little scream, and Wick, listing like a ship, shuffles closer to the bear, waving his lantern so that it hisses ominously. But the animal stands fast, greedy for food. "Get!" Wick yells. "Get, Goddammit! I'm a man! Get!"

The bear weaves in and out of the lantern's dull amber light, and Bev can see a white chest mark, and patches of skin grinning in crescents on its haunches where the fur is rubbed away. The creature falters, grunting and shaking its head back and forth, and it's then that Wick, his arm curled like a girl's, throws the lantern in a narrow, high arc. But it falls short, sputtering on the packed earth of the site.

In the strange, snapping light, Wick's arms flutter rigidly. "I will not hide my face from you!" he screams at the bear, which feints away, then close, in a kind of dance.

"Goddamn you!" Bev cries at the bear, too, and lunges through the tall grass, her flannel nightgown flapping against her legs like a flag. "Goddamn you!"

She lurches to where Wick stands amidst the debris from the lantern, bone-white arms raised over his head. In the spastic light from the broken lamp, his face is radiant.

Swaying, the bear eyes them both and snorts, giving off a sour, fusty breath, then drops to all fours and lumbers away. "You tell me where God went!" Wick yells after the bear, his voice quavering, but the creature is already indistinguishable from the trees, black on black, and they are left gaping at each other as the lantern dies at their feet.

"Be careful of the glass, Wick," Bev finally says.

"The lamp," Wick murmurs.

They stare at each other. Bev can hear the birches with their stick-lady arms, moving in the dark, and the patient night lament of the crickets. She reaches across the space between them, taking his hand. His grip surprises her with its strength. "Where do you think God has gone?" she says, her voice trembling. She wants to hear him speak again, but even more than this she wants to know what he will say.

Wick peers at her, then snorts. In the last flickers of the lamp his face has twisted free of its sagging contours into a riddle of near-contempt. "*Pah!* He's gone." His voice a bleary singsong, he turns from her, then whips back around. "I have seen."

"Wick?"

"The black priests—ask *them*," he says. "Mystical night. You ask *them*." Still clutching her hand, Wick starts toward the tent.

Bev allows herself to be pulled along, her face burning as though she has been slapped. "Wick!" she cries, tugging at his hand to make him slow down. Their progress is uneven, and in the darkness the twigs and stones lie in wait. "I don't understand. What are you saying?"

Outside the tent he pulls away from her and ducks awkwardly inside. Bev stands perfectly still, her feet stinging. When she creeps into the tent, Wick is already rolled into his sleeping bag. "We'll talk tomorrow, then," she says, sitting down heavily and touching her bare feet. They are torn, bleeding a little. "We have plenty of time to talk."

For almost an hour, Bev sits propped against her pillow and bedroll, regarding her husband in the strange blue light of the tent and fighting the urge to wake him. Outside, the evergreens sigh. She presses her hands close to her face, understanding on some level that Wick has provided her with a key. But it is so incomprehensible to her that she wraps her arms about her knees and, in confused fearfulness, rocks quietly.

She thinks about a time years ago, during her pregnancy. They were eating breakfast in their old yellow kitchen, and Wick kept leaning over, placing his long fingers flat against her belly, his voice throaty with promise: "We're in this together, Bevvy!" She had been so afraid, but then Linda was born, and their daughter was beautiful.

Bev stares at the hatched weave of the tent, which is grimy, but in a pleasant, utilitarian way; it smells of pine and earth. *This is the world into which we are born*, Bev reasons drowsily; *how bad can it be?* Just before she sleeps, she remembers the lawn chairs she packed: she will set them out tomorrow, and they will have coffee. They will talk.

She wakes hours later. For a moment she lies on her side and watches Wick sleep, the back of his head and his seamed, fragile neck. She lifts herself out of the tent; her shoulder is stiff, bent strangely while she slept, but if she moves slowly, languorously, she can make a fire for coffee; she can tend the fire until it is right and the coffee bubbles. The tent is still quiet, and so she pours herself a cup and walks to where the trail angles down to the lake.

How like a cathedral it is, the green boughs arching over the path. The light out here is dusky; Bev takes a breath. She will start with the bear, she thinks, its cracked-hazel eyes and broken claws. She will remind Wick that he protected her. *You were so brave*, she might say; only then will she mention anything about God. Casually, of course. So casually. She cannot admit, even to herself, how important it is that her husband explains.

She realizes then that she cannot wait. Clutching her mug, she jogs back up the hill to their little tent, which is still quiet and closed. "Wick, wake up!" she calls, breathless, half-singing the words, the way she used to wake Linda. Laughing with relief: "Let's clear this up, dearie!" Bev pulls back the tent flap and sees that her husband lies flat on his back, staring up at the rough cloth of the tent, a trace of drool gleaming wet on his chin. "Wick! Good morning. The bear! Remember the bear?"

He swivels his head to face her, his eyes empty.

"The bear, the bear, you saved me, remember?" Her voice pleads against the half-light in his eyes and the dull crust ringing his mouth. "I saw you. I saw you. Hey!" she yells. "You come back now. Take it *back*." Bev sets down the mug with a thud, hot coffee spatting her wrist.

Wick's eyes swim past hers. His lips are parted, and Bev can see his tongue, thick and gleaming. It looks sly. Sinking beside him on her knees, she begins to beat at his chest and arms with her open hands. He looks away from her, not seeming to register the blows.

"Enough! Enough! Don't leave me this way!" She slaps him until her hands sting. "Dear God," she says finally, resting her head against him. He does not resist. The tent flap has fallen closed and the two of them are trapped in blue twilight. "Wick," she says. She wonders where, in the hierarchy of sins, hate falls.

Outside their tent, the birches sway like dancers. The lake moves on stones, its surface corrugated with waves that are blue on green. Bev knows this. She can picture the herons that nest along the shore, and she can picture herself in five years, ten. Wick's heart will continue beating—she is certain—in the months and years stretching ahead for them both, his changed spirit unreachable within a body that persists. She can hear it now, his heart, that reliable arbiter of corporeal health, and its dull tattoo does not comfort her where she lies, head pressed out of habit against his long and elegant chest.

The Decline of Pigeons
in the Natural World

It's rush hour and the taillights ahead of Gayle are a long, bright river. A few times she tries Peter on his cell phone but hangs up at the low buzz of his recorded voice. "You leave a message, now," the phone instructs. *Hurry*, she begs the traffic. He doesn't know that his daughter's been stranded at ballet; why would he? It's not his night. Thank God she and Emme exchanged numbers that first dinner out; it had been a way to bond with her new boyfriend's daughter. And just where in the hell is Lynn? Terrific mother, that one; by the time Gayle pulls up in front of the Elegante Ballet School, she has worked herself into a state of joyous indignation.

Emme waits in the dark doorway alone, arms crossed and the froth of her tutu scratching pink beneath the hem of a sheepskin coat. "You came!" The girl sounds borderline frantic, scrambling into the passenger seat when Gayle throws open the door.

Emme is a petite ten-year-old with narrow shoulders and muted coloring: nothing like Peter, his bulk that of the aging athlete, hair as dark as otter pelt. Emme's slight frame must come from her mother, and every time Gayle thinks of this she is mildly discomfited. Her own body is amply constructed, as dimpled and white as a pudding.

"I came," Gayle says, and touches the girl's arm before swinging the car back into the street.

Emme's puffy around the eyes and a crust of snot has formed beneath her nose. But she's trying to be cool: she crosses her legs in their thick pink tights and thumps a foot intermittently against the dash.

"You okay?" Gayle glances sidelong at the girl, at the red spots darkening her cheeks.

"Sure."

Something in the child's posture—the dignified, patient set of her spine—makes Gayle's heart ache. "I'm glad you called," she says.

They are in a bewildering intersection of strip malls, feverishly festive: electric candy canes and hairy-tinsel Santas. The van in front of them is so large that Gayle can't see beyond this moment, the small circle of light and warmth they occupy in Gayle's sensible single-woman car.

"*You* came," Emme says with such warmth that it takes Gayle a moment to answer, her own voice thick as she says what she is supposed to: something about Lynn having a good reason to be late, that these things happen.

"I tried to call her," Emme says.

"I know you did, honey." And then she can't help herself: "It's not okay, you waiting outside all this time."

"It's not mom's fault," Emme says quickly, and Gayle amends, equally fast: "Of course! If she could have made it, she would have." They are catching the green lights now, bucketing through the intersections. A crucial misstep, badmouthing Lynn. *Younger children always defend their mothers,* Gayle thinks; it's a perk of parenthood, however undeserved.

"So do you like ballet?" she says after an awkward interval. Her voice is too bright. Like the other adults in Emme's life, probably. Like Lynn.

But Emme turns from the window to look at her. "It's okay," she says. "The girls are kinda mean. They go to a different school than me."

Gayle turns down the volume on the radio. "Kids can be mean at this age," she agrees. "Especially girls. I used to have problems with this girl in my homeroom. Kimmie something. I used to dread that ten minutes every morning." Gayle speaks airily; she hasn't thought about her seventh-grade homeroom for years. No, that's not true, exactly, but it feels okay, telling Emme this. "When you get to be my age, none of this will matter."

"Really?"

"Really." Gayle is pleased that the child seems to believe her.

"Huh." Emme looks straight ahead, picking thoughtfully at her nose. "I like the dancing part," she finally says.

They are close, now: another fifteen, twenty minutes, and they'll be at Gayle's townhouse. "We can bake when we get to my place," Gayle says, remembering cookie dough—sugar, the kind that comes in a tube—waiting in the fridge. "The place will smell nice when your dad comes over."

But when they get there they don't even turn on the oven. Still in their coats, giggling, they squeeze onto stools at the narrow breakfast bar, slitting open the tube and eating dough raw, with plastic spoons.

"I like it here!" Emme says. Tears have dried on her face, giving it a curiously dappled look, but her eyes are bright.

"Good," Gayle says.

—

"Lynn's mother—Emme's grandma—she's been sick," Peter says later that night. He has mixed them a pitcher of martinis dry as wood but Gayle has barely touched hers, so agitated is she by the evening she has shared with Emme. Gayle glances into the den, where Emme sleeps, wearing one of Gayle's old Michigan State T-shirts, one thin arm thrown over her head. "Lynn's got her hands full right now; sometimes she gets depressed. Things slip through the cracks."

"Like remembering she has a daughter?"

Peter sighs, massaging his temples. "I already talked to her about what happened."

"You *talked* to her?" Gayle interrupts. "What'd you say? 'Hey, honey, you ditched our kid'? And this girl, this *infant*, meanwhile—"

"Listen," Peter says. "She made a mistake. Do we have to talk about this right now?" He tries a grin.

"I think Emme liked dinner, don't you?" Gayle takes a swift drink. Emme had been so hungry: after the cookie dough, they had between them, in a ritual, workmanlike fashion, dispatched a pint of ice cream; two heels of good bread, spread thickly with peanut butter and honey; and the last stale Girl Scout cookies. "Does Lynn even feed the child?"

"Gayle. Please." Peter rubs his closed eyes with the pads of his fingers. "I'm not making excuses for her."

"It sounds like you are." Although Peter has insisted that he initiated the divorce—"We just wanted different things," he has told Gayle—a habit of wistfulness clings to him when the subject of Lynn comes up. One night when he'd been drinking Peter let it slip how he'd lost his "beautiful girl." Lynn was the best thing that ever happened to him, he'd said sleepily, and then, apparently sober enough, hastily added, "Until you, of course."

"How sick is the grandma?" Gayle says.

Peter takes a deep breath. "Lynn's mother has lung cancer, Gayle. Lynn's gonna have to stay with her for awhile, in Wisconsin. I'll stay out at the house." His lip juts, a petulant child.

Gayle sips her drink. She doesn't care about Lynn's mother, her sad and rotting lungs. "Why can't Emme stay at your place?"

"She's got school, Gayle," Peter says.

"But isn't that kind of disruptive?" Gayle says. "For you, I mean?"

"It's only 'til Christmas."

"Well, for us, then."

"Comes with the territory of being a parent," Peter says. "You gotta do what you gotta do." But his voice is unhappy. He stands abruptly and moves to the window, his broad back to her.

Gayle's seen the split-level in the suburbs where Peter once lived with his family. It doesn't seem like him; it's hard to imagine him there now.

"How long have you known about this . . . plan?" She can't help herself; sometimes she wonders how often he and Lynn talk.

"Shit," he says, and buries his head in his fists.

Gayle moves behind him and massages his shoulders. "Oh, honey. Honey. I'm sorry. What a pain in the ass." Outside her window, the sky is bleached pure by the city's lights. "Well, maybe I can come out from Chicago, visit you two. We can—I don't know, go to Ponderosa or something." She means for Peter to laugh and is gratified when he does. The first time she met Emme—what was it? A month ago?—they had shared dinner in an orange plastic booth at Ponderosa. But what she's really thinking about are the delicate planes of the girl's face, the shy tuck of her chin when she is pleased. "Well, here we all are," Peter had said, gazing around the table, smiling in befuddled amusement at the two of them, their faces open to him, and laughing.

—

Gayle cannot recall a time when she has not wanted children of her own, on whom she could lavish attention; by twelve, she had already planned the pink confection of her own wedding. The fourth child of five, the only girl, she could sit cross-legged for hours on her neatly made bed, planning, in the room she shared with two brothers popular enough to be absent well into the night. Her children would be named Hope and Davey, she decided; they liked purple and red, respectively; they both clamored for a cat named Sean. And then she grew up and waited for it all to happen. For the longest time it didn't occur to her that she might not meet someone in time to start a family of her own. Her girlfriends, married off one by one, have borne children; some are already divorced, and a few have made starts on second marriages. They tell her she's too picky when it comes to men. "I don't need to date just anyone," she has said. "I can afford to wait for the right guy." She spoke confidently; she looks younger than her thirty-eight years; she has a good job as a consultant and dresses well. But, saying it, her heart burned.

When she met Peter, at a Halloween party, it wasn't exactly fireworks, but then she'd been in a bad mood. It had been a terrible week. Tuesday she'd missed a deadline at work; on Friday she was clocked by her own cupboard door so that a shiner bloomed overnight. If she hadn't promised that she'd bring hummus to the party, she wouldn't have gone at all, but Gayle made her own statement by wearing street clothes and nursing a scotch amidst the assorted vampires and sexy nurses. When Peter plunked himself down on the arm of the sofa, she hadn't noticed his Levi's and plain-blue button-down.

"No costume?" His expression was mocking.

Oh, shut up, she thought. "I've got a costume," she said, and stuffed a throw pillow under her peasant blouse so that the fabric strained, sheer and pink as flesh pulled taut. "Connie Corleone." She stuck out her chin, daring him to comment: on the hard bulge of the pillow, on the broken capillaries in her battered eye. If she'd been in a better mood she would have helped him out: "*Godfather I*, you know?" But she said nothing, just stared at him, waiting.

"Oh, yeah, leave the gun, take the cannoli," he'd said, so good-naturedly that it was then that she began to imagine he might have potential. She checked his ring finger, providentially bare; she even forgave him when, encouraged by her surprised, barking laugh, he'd cocked his hand like a gun and said, "Bang bang."

He called her the next morning. They went out for coffee and then, when that was painless enough, a movie and dinner. He was sweet—his every action characterized by a genuine, shambling courtesy—and had probably once been boyishly handsome. His broad, frank face was now only slightly mottled, and though he carried some extra pounds, when they went to bed on that first real movie date the sex was remarkably good. When Peter touches her, all these weeks later, the skin on the insides of her arms, her thighs, still draws up in exultation, and at those times she thinks, *My God, I love men!*

Of course he has baggage. This is to be expected of a man his age: he is past forty, after all. There is the marriage, which dissolved last year, and the ex-wife, Lynn. But it was nice to be with someone who seemed to want to be with her. You don't want to alarm people, you don't want to try too hard, but with Peter, Gayle didn't find herself squelching the familiar, anxious need. If anything, she was more nervous about pleasing the child. "I have a daughter—a little girl," Peter had said that first dinner together, turning his wineglass around and around, until Gayle covered his hand with her own, touched that he might be nervous about such disclosure when, in fact, she could hardly believe her luck.

She's always thought she'd like to have a girlchild first; Hope, phantom Hope, was the elder of the two.

—

"What are you working on, Emme?" Gayle sits down at the kitchen table, where Emme, barricaded behind a stack of books, furiously scribbles on note cards.

Gayle drove out to the house this afternoon, her arms loaded with groceries from Peter's favorite health food store in the city. "So you won't go hungry," she'd said. Peter rifled through the veggie chips, bran cookies, and cold pasta salad, his mouth slack with appreciation. "Real food!" he'd exclaimed. He's been living at the house for less than a week.

"A report," Emme says now, and lays her head on her arm. "Passenger pigeons."

"Passenger pigeons. Like *The Bird Man of Alcatraz*?"

Emme looks blank. "They're extinct," she says.

"Oh." Gayle sits down and pulls one of the books toward her, an encyclopedia with a missing cover. Peter had told her on the phone that since he moved out here, his daughter has been uncommunicative. The first night he heard her crying.

"She's probably worried about her grandma," Gayle had said, relishing the opportunity to speculate. "Are they close?"

"I think she thinks I don't want to be here," Peter said. His voice was a misery of guilt.

Did he? It was hard to tell with men sometimes. Surely he loved his daughter, but Peter has told Gayle he never felt at home in the suburbs. "Of course you want to be there," Gayle said. "We're both there for your girl."

"It's hard to write," Emme complains now. She turns her face into her arm, speaking so that the words blur together. "I went online and found things, but my teacher says we need stuff from print resources, too. These books are hard."

"Does your mom usually help with your homework?" Gayle asks casually, pulling another book from the pile. It's some sort of oral history.

"I'm not a *baby*." Emme looks up, fair brows knit, warning outrage. "I don't need my mother."

"Of course you don't," Gayle says, her voice happier than she means it to sound. "For homework, I mean." She turns the oral history over in her hands. "This one looks okay." She can't remember, really, what it's like to be ten. "What are you learning?"

Emme's expression brightens. "There were all these pigeons and now they're gone," she says, sitting up.

"Huh." When Gayle opens the book Emme slips from her chair and leans against her. Gayle ruffles the girl's ponytail. "Pretty," she says, for even in the florescent glare of the kitchen, the child's hair possesses lights of red and gold. "We should do it up sometime."

"Really?" Emme comes as close to squealing as Gayle has ever heard her. "I have my mom's hair," she says. "Mom's really beautiful."

A timer light in the next room winks and Gayle feels the need to stand. "I'm sure she is." Moving to the door to peer into the darkness, she buttons her cardigan. She'd dressed carefully this morning: Peter has told her he likes her in blue. She wonders, suddenly, if to Emme she looks like nothing so much as a middle-aged woman. Lynn had Emme quite early, she remembers. "It's late, munchkin," she says abruptly. "Why don't you get ready for bed? We'll talk pigeons later."

"Okay."

But Emme drifts into the living room and turns on the TV.

"Bed. Okay?" Gayle glances at the clock and feels a prick of irritation. Peter's been gone for more than an hour, to pick out a rental movie for them to watch later tonight. So what's the deal: she's supposed to be the bad guy and put Emme to bed?

When Emme drags upstairs, Gayle returns to the book. Emme has marked a chapter where a woman talks about the harvesting of passenger pigeons, when she was a young girl in the late 1870s. At that time, the birds were still legion. *At least 1.1 million birds were shipped to market from the Michigan harvest alone*, the woman recalled. *They were considered a delicacy, until the market was glutted; then they were fed to the hogs.*

"Hi, babe." Peter is home finally, a DVD in each hand.

When he leans over to kiss her, she smells beer on his breath. "I see they have a bar at Blockbuster now," Gayle says, averting her face. "Your daughter is upstairs, waiting to be put to bed." She shrugs her shoulders, determined not to be a shrew, but cannot resist saying, "It might have been nice if you'd spent some time with her tonight."

"O-kaaaaay." Peter, hands raised in surrender, heads upstairs, and Gayle glares at the pages in front of her.

Sulfur pots were used to suffocate the birds, the woman, Elsa Gross, remembers. *Men went about with sticks, knocking down the birds' nests; others chopped down the trees or broke off branches laden with birds. The pigeons were terrified, and their cackling combined into a roar that could be heard a mile away.*

Gayle snaps the book shut, staring out the kitchen window but then closing her eyes to the dark and ugly house next door. When she opens them Peter is standing there.

"Emme wants to say good night," he tells her apologetically.

"She does?"

Peter grins at her. "What can I say? She likes you." When Gayle stands, he pats her butt. "I'm sorry I kept you waiting, Gayle. It's just been a hell of a week. Thanks for keeping her company tonight." He smiles at her, his brilliant smile. "You're good with her. A natural."

Gayle nods, fighting and then giving in to a smile herself. All right, so Peter sounds a little drunk. She'd be drunk, too, if she was commuting from Bumfuck every day. "You didn't mention my sweater," she says, canting her hip and assuming an expression of mock petulance. She pushes the book to one side of the table.

"Oh, you look good in blue, all right," Peter says. He pats her butt again as she squeezes past him.

"Don't start the movie without me!" Gayle takes the stairs two at a time. "Good night," she calls when she reaches the top. It's dark in the hall, and Gayle fumbles open the wrong door—what looks like a sewing room—before finding Emme's: purple foam stars stuck to the door and a twin bed against the far wall, the child a small hill in the blankets.

"Good night, Gayle," Emme pipes. "I'm glad you're here." Her voice is muffled by a rustling, and then a light clicks on. Gayle blinks in the sudden brightness. Emme sits in a nest of pink blankets, shading her eyes. "Come in," she says.

The room is small, smaller even than the room Gayle once shared with her brothers, with a tiny window that's almost a porthole. On the walls panda wallpaper has been layered over with posters: horses, rainbows. A Doors poster stands out.

Gayle sits on the edge of the bed. "Jim Morrison fan, huh?" she says, smiling. Emme looks blank, and Gayle nods at the poster.

"I made my dad pick out something for me," Emme says. "The other girls, they talk about music all the time. Dad says they're cool. The Doors." She searches Gayle's face. "Are they? Cool?"

"Very," Gayle says, and pats the pillow. "Lie down, now, huh?"

"Okay." Emme lies down but doesn't turn out the light.

"*You're* cool, Gayle. I'm glad you're here."

"Me, too." Gayle hugs the child, enfolding her thin shoulders. "Sleep tight, okay?"

"Don't let the bedbugs bite." Emme starts to turn over and then sits up again. "I'm glad you're here," she repeats. "You're nice." She is wearing a shiny nightgown, patterned with seahorses, that bunches crisply under her arms. "At first I was mad when Mom sent Dad away, but just think, if that hadn't happened, I wouldn't have met you. Right?" Emme furrows her brow.

Wasn't it the other way around; hadn't Peter called off the marriage? *We just wanted different things.* "You're tired," Gayle says. "You get some sleep now."

"Can you stay the night?" Emme's voice already sounds sleepier.

"Oh, honey, I can't do that. But I'll see you soon."

"Okay. Promise?" Emme turns over and Gayle suddenly sees that the girl clutches a corduroy bear. She turns off the light, then doesn't move, sitting sentinel until she hears Emme's breathing lull into a gentle snore. She loves the quiet of the room, and sitting so near the child, Gayle feels joy move warm into her arms and up her spine, cupping her neck and the back of her head.

Peter must come fetch her, calling from the dark doorway: "Come on, Gayle, I'm ready for you. Let's watch some movies."

—

"So where was Lynn the night Emme had ballet?" Gayle says. They are about to start the movie; Peter has poured them each a glass of wine and filled a red plastic bowl with chips. She fiddles with the pearled button on her cardigan.

"Miss Nosy," Peter teases. He puts his arm around her as he aims the remote.

"No. Peter. Listen to me."

"*You're* my girl," Peter says. He drinks deeply of his wine, and winks at her. "Why would we spend our night talking about Lynn?" He waves his arm, indicating the house. "In this *palace*—"

Gayle starts to laugh. "C'mon, it's not so bad."

"I just want you to know that I am not responsible for the decorating here." They're both laughing now.

Children become confused, Gayle reminds herself. And who knows what lies Lynn has told her daughter. "That's not what I hear. The Doors, huh?"

"Youthful indiscretion." Peter pulls her to him, kissing her brow bone, and then leans back. "I have made mistakes. I enjoy a drink. I like my job. I have an appreciation for women. But I've *learned* from my mistakes. You—" and he traces the arc of Gayle's cheek with a thick forefinger—"you understand a person's potential."

Gayle gazes back at him; his eyes are as round and guileless as pennies. When she settles against his bulk, the light from the television plays against her face, speaking to her of domestic comfort, of being at home in the world.

Gayle means to drive back to the city later that night, but after the movie it's past one, and Peter convinces her to stay. "The weather could turn nasty," he says from the depths of the couch. "You could get caught in a snowstorm."

"What about Emme?" Gayle says. She's moved out of his arms and has started lacing up her shoes. "And Lynn?"

"Emme thinks you're great. And if Lynn takes issue, she can talk to me about it." Peter sits up and rubs his eyes.

Gayle moves to the kitchen table, where the stack of books catches her eye. "This book is too mature for Emme," she says, picking up the oral history. "Did Lynn get these for her?"

"Don't change the subject." Peter comes up behind her, matching his hips to hers. "Did I tell you you're a knockout in blue?"

"Okay, okay." Gayle laughs.

It seems kind of weird, sleeping in Lynn's house, but on some level Gayle is relieved. It's hard to think of driving home at this hour. Peter goes to take a shower, and Gayle wanders through to the kitchen. In the refrigerator she finds the pasta salad she brought Peter, along with a carton of milk past its sell date and a Tupperware container of what might be soup. Jesus! No wonder the kid is thin. Gayle rips open one of the packets of bran cookies from the health food store and, chewing, climbs the stairs to stand outside the bathroom. The shower's still running. When she ducks her head inside, she can hear Peter singing.

"Almost done in here?" Gayle glances at the mirror but she can't see herself through the clouds of steam.

"Five minutes, babe."

"Okay, five minutes." As she starts to withdraw, her hand slips across something smooth—a gown, or a robe, maybe, hanging on the back of the door.

Gayle can just see the shape of Peter through the opaque glass; she imagines the water running in sheets across the expanse of his back. Next to him, she thinks, she is almost petite.

"Bye," she says, grabbing the gown. She takes it with her to the bedroom—the gloomy, green master bedroom—where she shoves aside Peter's suitcase, gaping open on the unmade bed, and strips out of her sweater, her jeans. She pulls on the gown—it is a gown, after all, with narrow silk straps and a shy border of lace. It smells like Lynn. Musky, salty. With some effort Gayle gets the thing over her hips. She moves to the mirror to see, steeling herself, but she doesn't look bad. Not too bad, the silk or satin or whatever it is stretched shiny over her belly. Her arms are nice, milky and soft but with a little definition, no dents in the upper flesh yet and Gayle smiles, twisting at the waist, preening.

When the fabric rips in a long crack along the seam, she isn't prepared; it's all she can do not to scream at the sight of her flesh, bursting through the tear.

Gayle rips off the gown and kicks it under the bed. When Peter comes in, minutes later, he finds her under the covers, dressed in one of the Oxford shirts she pulled from his suitcase.

"Cute," he says. And not too much later, he slips his hand inside the shirt.

"No, no," she says at first, kissing and then removing his hands, which are surprisingly narrow, though when he persists she allows him to roll on top of her. She cannot see his face in the dark, but as he rocks above her, the springs of Lynn's bed clicking rhythmically, Gayle is reassured. Afterwards she draws him close and listens, vigilant, in case there should be a sound from her lover's daughter, sleeping just down the hall.

—

The next morning, Sunday, Gayle means to leave before Emme wakes up, but ends up lingering over her coffee. It's so pleasant in the kitchen; Peter has the radio going and the sun makes watery patterns on the wall. Gayle picks up the oral history again. It doesn't menace her today; it's a curiosity.

"Listen to this," she says to Peter. Already dressed in jeans and a flannel shirt, he is shuffling around the kitchen, unloading the dishwasher and making a second pot of coffee. "There used to be so many passenger pigeons, they'd darken the sky when they flew over," Gayle reads aloud. She pauses for effect. "They'd *darken the sky*, just completely blot out the sun. Isn't that wild? In 1810, Audubon saw a flock in Kentucky that was so big it took three days to pass overhead."

"The bird guy?" Peter pours himself another cup of coffee.

"Uh-huh. They blotted out the sun, for Chrissakes."

"That's a lot of birds." Peter's voice is teasing.

"No, listen. Really. Here's the weird part: in 1880, there were still passenger pigeons in the millions. By the end of the decade, if you saw 175 birds together, that was a big deal. The last one died in a zoo, in 1914."

"1914: the last pigeon, and Archduke Ferdinand," Peter says. "May they rest in peace."

"Oh, shut up!" Gayle laughs, and throws the book at him; when he catches it, one-handed, she laughs harder.

"We could go back to bed for a little," Peter says. Gayle looks at him. His hair crests like a boy's, but his shoulders are wide as an ox cart. "Just for a little." Leaning over, grinning, he squeezes her bare thigh; she's still wearing his shirt.

"Emme!" Gayle says, clapping her legs together. The girl is standing in the doorway, her shiny pink nightgown hanging stiff to her ankles.

Peter jerks around and grabs his coffee. "Hi, sweetie!"

Emme smiles at them both. "You're here!" she says to Gayle, genuine pleasure in her voice. "Are we gonna do something today?" Emme looks from one to the other. "Together? Please?"

"Yes, Gayle, can you stay the day?" Peter, managing to look both flustered and plaintive, steps to the other side of the kitchen table. "Come out with us somewhere? My treat!"

"I'd love to," Gayle says without pause, holding the shirt closed over her breasts. "Listen. Emme. Let me get dressed and then you and I can do your hair, okay?"

Emme squeals and Peter looks relieved. "Okay, Emme," he says. "Breakfast first." Gayle leaves them in the kitchen, and when she runs up the stairs, the carpet is rough, thrilling against her bare feet.

—

In the upstairs bathroom, Emme sits on the sink counter, thumping the heels of her socked feet against the cabinets. It's another small room, made smaller by foil wallpaper and dark cabinetry, but Gayle's spirits are winged, her chest spacious. "I made that," Emme says, poking at a ceramic whale painted eggplant red. "See? It's for the toothbrushes."

"Ah," Gayle says, and ties another ribbon in Emme's hair. She found them in a kitchen drawer; Gayle thinks the rich, shiny green will look good in the girl's hair. She holds up a mirror so that Emme can see the back of her head, the straight and tender white part, the glossy ribbons.

"Help me pick out something to wear!" Emme slides off the counter and pulls Gayle to her room, to her packed closet.

"My mom bought me some new clothes last week," Emme says. "Before she left." She tugs at the sleeve of a tiny black sweater that clings to the hanger like moss. "Or this: do you like this one?" The blouse is cut from a shiny, almost opalescent material, some sort of shimmering purple satin lit with green highlights. The buttons are faceted like little diamonds. "Mom said these were cool."

Gayle heaves aside the new clothing, hangers scratching along the wooden pole. "What about this?" She pulls out a nubbly pink sweater, appliqued with kittens, that has been smashed into a far corner.

"Gayle, that's *old*." Emme's laugh is bright as water. "I wore that when I was a little girl!"

You are a little girl, Gayle wants to say, but she holds the sweater up beside Emme's face and nods thoughtfully. "Look at how the pink brings out the color in your cheeks," she says in her most authoritative voice. "And it contrasts with the ribbons, see?" She leads Emme to a round wall mirror, standing behind her and holding up the sweater, which *does* look pretty: soft and sweet. And won't Emme have a lifetime to wear black, after all?

"Are you sure?" Emme says, but she preens a little in the mirror, canting her head to one side.

When they get downstairs, Peter is at the kitchen table, sorting through a stack of brochures.

"Gayle says the ribbons *contrast*." Emme smoothes her sweater and then pats primly at her hair.

Peter glances up and smiles distractedly. "Great," he says, tapping the brochures. "Look what I found in the junk drawer. We've got all this stuff about museums. Want to go into the city?"

"I'm game," Gayle says, but Emme claps her hands and shouts, "Enchanted Castle! Enchanted Castle!"

Peter rolls his eyes good-naturedly, and Emme says breathlessly, "It's an *entertainment complex*! It's great, Gayle: there's rides, games—you'll like it!"

She doesn't, of course, at least not when they drive up, Emme leaning over from the backseat and the sunroof open. Even with the three of them cramped together in Peter's car, she's happy, though. It's unseasonably warm, the wind blending their hair and they are laughing, the music cranked. It might rain later, even snow. But for now the sun emerges periodically, lighting Emme's thin white hand where it grips Gayle's shoulder. The child's ribbons flutter.

Enchanted Castle occupies one long arm of a V-shaped strip mall located a few towns over; castle battlements have been effected in one dimension of brick over the flat strip-mall roof, and the plate-glass doors are cloudy with fingerprints. When they pass through, Gayle pokes Peter and nods at a sign:

All hats must be worn with bills forward (no hoods or bandannas).

"Gang problems? Here?"

"Maybe," Peter says. Inside, the din is appalling. The pounding bass of an old Blues Brothers song mixes with beeps and squawks from the rows of video games. The noise is like a living thing, trapped beneath the low ceiling of black-painted acoustic tile.

But Emme is grinning. "Daddy! Let's play Skeeball!" she cries, and Gayle experiences a surge of tenderness, for the girl or Peter, she can't tell. She's never heard Peter called Daddy before.

"Sure, sure," Peter says, and they establish themselves at the foot of a wooden Skeeball ramp.

Gayle watches Peter put his hand on Emme's shoulder, coaching her throw; Emme pretends to wind up like a pitcher. She's a funny, kind child, Gayle thinks, not so jaded that she can't admit to having fun with an adult. When it becomes evident that they're going to play until they can collect a decent prize, Gayle decides to explore.

"I'll be back, you two," she says, and they both turn and smile at her. She wanders past a mirrored corner where the Krazy Kars are tethered, painted in thick red-and-gold enamel. The miniature golf course has drawn a family to its peeling gilt gates for a photo and as she passes, Gayle gives a little nod. The parents wave broadly, saluting her; to them she's a fellow mother, enduring the Enchanted Castle for the sake of the kids. Gayle's chest swells and she waves back. By the time she returns to the Skeeball, the Blues Brothers have segued into hip-hop.

Emme, face burnished with glee, greets Gayle with a shriek. "Let's go get a prize!" she cries, and drags Gayle to the "store" where the winnings are kept. There's the usual cheap carnival fare, including mirrored photos of sports figures and minor country-and-western singers. Jewelry is laid out in a glass case meant to confer value.

"God preserve us," Peter says, but he smiles as he helps his daughter pick out the least gaudy of the necklaces.

They have their picture taken then, the three of them, in a narrow booth. The machine grunts and chugs, then spits out the strip of photos. There is Peter, looking fake-stern and fatherly; Emme mugs, pointing at her new necklace; Gayle has her arms around them both, her round, shiny face so happy that it looks, in the grainy black-and-white photos, lit from within.

Emme carefully tears the photo strip into three: each of them can keep a picture, she declares. "Thank you, sweetie," Gayle says, examining her photo carefully. She looks all right, doesn't she? Almost pretty. Gayle slips the photo into her wallet.

"So who's hungry?" Peter asks.

"I am!" Emme says. "I want a hot dog. A hot dog with mustard."

Gayle, ravenous, feels as though she could eat the world. She links her arm in Peter's, and they watch—*fondly*, Gayle thinks—as Emme scampers ahead of them.

"I can't believe I'm saying this, but I love Enchanted Castle." Gayle starts to laugh. "Peter, I'm having so much fun!"

Peter smiles, studying a menu placard. "Stick with us, babe. We know how to have a good time."

"She's a great kid," Gayle says.

"So are you," Peter says. "No, really," he adds, giving her arm a squeeze. "You're good with her, Gayle. You're special." Eyes cast down in fluttery expectation, she waits for him to tell her more, but he's staring at the menu, tapping his teeth. "Jesus, I'm starving!" he finally says. "I think even this shit will taste okay!"

The King's Table serves chicken patties, hamburgers, hot dogs on the King's Bread. The hot dog line is shortest: just a group of girls Emme's age, clowning around. One of them is striking, with a hard, pretty face and hair so black the highlights are almost blue; she shakes her head with the authority of a grown woman.

Emme sees them and her face closes. "I'd rather have chicken," she says abruptly, and heads toward that line.

"No King's Bread?" Gayle calls after her, meaning to joke, but Emme doesn't turn around. Gayle glances at Peter and he shrugs. "I'll have chicken, too, I guess," she says finally, and joins Emme in line.

"Hey, you," Gayle says. "Everything okay?"

"I'm just tired." Emme looks glum.

"*Nice* light fixtures," Gayle says, because the wall sconces really are absurd, paper blown upwards in front of a light bulb to simulate flames. Emme's face remains stony. "Okay," Gayle says. "That's okay."

Emme chooses a table in a corner far from the crowd and near a karaoke machine, the music so loud that they can't talk and so eat quickly, taking their food in hasty, gulping bites. Emme's mood seems to have brought Peter down—he's sullen now, glancing at his watch—but Gayle, chewing her sandwich, decides that she is still happy. She knows how it is with teens, or almost-teens, and with men, too. The flurry of moods, the impatience.

She winks reassuringly at Emme, and when Peter's cell phone rings she smiles at him in commiseration. "Don't you hate those things?"

But he is already on his feet, phone to ear and mouthing: "It's work. I'll be back in a sec."

"Finish your meal," Gayle says to him, meaning to be . . . what? Motherly? Kind? She wonders about this later. "The phone can wait."

"Excuse me, it can*not*," Peter says loudly over the music. He hurries off, exclaiming, "I'm sorry!" to whoever is on the phone.

Gayle's cheeks burn, but she makes herself look at Emme, who stands now, too. "I have to go to the bathroom," the girl announces.

"I could come," Gayle says, but Emme shakes her head mutinously. Her face is red, like Gayle imagines her own must be, those same spots of anger and humiliation high in her cheeks.

"I don't need help, if that's what you think." Pulling at her sweater, Emme marches off to the bathroom.

Gayle watches her go, then turns to finish her sandwich. She is suddenly forlorn but the chicken is greasy and satisfying, washed down with coffee almost white with cream. She steals a few fries from Emme's plate, then a few more. The music is painfully loud. When the girl doesn't return from the bathroom and Peter, across the room, talking animatedly on his cell, doesn't meet her eye, she dumps the remainder of the fries onto her own plate, eating them in bunches, three or four pinched together like stems in a bouquet. She extracts the photo from her wallet. The smiling faces reassure her.

When she has cleared everyone's plate, she glances at her watch; Emme's been in the bathroom for a good ten minutes. Peter finally catches her eye, his eyebrows raised in question. Gayle points to the bathroom and then, suddenly uneasy, stands and pushes through a crowd of grammar school kids in identical red T-shirts.

The bathroom is pale yellow tile, a long, unclean room with the sinks and mirrors ranged on Gayle's left, the stalls to her right. At the far end Emme stands amidst the group of girls from the hot dog line, and at first Gayle thinks with a mix of relief and irritation that they're hanging out, that they've been hanging out all this time. For God's sake, has Emme been sneaking a cigarette?

"I've been worried," Gayle almost says, but then she sees the desperate set to Emme's face and the way the other girls surround her, circling with such scornful grace that Gayle finds herself mesmerized. No one seems to notice her, hand still on the door. Gayle registers the frisson of fine electric joy holding the circle together and she hears the grunting sound, just barely audible, that Emme makes, her head lowered. The girls sway their hips like much older girls—women, really, in their sheer blouses and short skirts, though they can't be much older than Emme. One reaches out and brushes Emme's shoulder, and a second girl bumps into Emme outright, snatching at her hair, while a third girl, the dark-haired one, hisses, "Oh, aren't we *pretty* today!"

"What the hell is going on here?" Gayle shouts, and in that

instant the spell is broken so that it's just three eleven-year-olds whirling to stare at her, faces blank and evasive. Emme has started to cry. One of the girls drops something to the floor and Gayle runs the length of the bathroom to pick it up, wanting to sob herself. It's Emme's necklace, broken, the cheap metal links torn. "Get out of here!" Gayle says, and she's surprised when the girls respond to her authority and leave, shuffling their Skechers, their narrow shoulders shifting.

Though one of them whispers, "*God*," just perceptibly.

"Get out of here if you know what's good for you!" Gayle screams.

When the door falls shut she grabs Emme and hugs her. "Are you okay?" The girl tenses, still weeping. "Do you know them?"

"They're in my ballet class," Emme says into Gayle's shoulder.

Gayle releases the girl and looks at her closely. "They didn't hurt you, did they?"

"No." Emme's stopped crying. Crouching, she retrieves a green ribbon from the floor and winds it carefully around her hand. "They're always like that."

"Goddamn little Barbie dolls," Gayle says. "Little bitches." Taking Emme by the shoulders, she pulls her up, less gently than she intends. "What did they say to you?"

"They said I dressed stupid, that I'm lame," Emme says. She looks down at her hand and opens her fingers so that the green ribbon flutters again to the floor. "They said I dressed like a baby." Emme's eyes widen in recognition. "You told me to wear this, Gayle! You said I looked cool!"

"You look fine, Emme. It's those girls who have a problem, not you."

"I should have worn the blouse my mom got me."

The cloudy, yellow tile bounces their voices back at them. "You look like a ten-year-old," Gayle says. "Which you are, the last time I checked. Those girls looked like hookers."

"They did not!" Emme screams. "You don't understand." She backs away from Gayle, paddling her hands in the air. "I hate you! You're fat and ugly, what do you know?"

When Gayle was Emme's age she was excluded and lonely, plain to the point of invisible. The girls back then used to call her fat. Fatty. Pork chop. "Come 'ere, Fatty! Wanta be friends?"

Gayle lifts her head and looks in the mirror. She is not an unattractive woman. Surely she has made something of her life.

The door opens then and a woman with a child by the hand peers in. "Is everything all right in here?" she says. She's younger than Gayle, with a soft, gentle face. Gayle takes in the loose dress, all primary colors, the cardigan sweater embroidered with birds; the woman looks like a kindergarten teacher, born to her role.

"We're fine," Gayle says tightly, and bends at the waist to retrieve the ribbon. "You looked pretty," she tells Peter's daughter. "Now you come with me."

—

Back at the table, Gayle gazes dully at Peter. She isn't sure he is a good parent. She isn't even sure, anymore, that he is a good man.

"I'm sorry," he whispers to Gayle. "I couldn't help that call. Damn office." He bends close, flicking at her ear with his tongue .

Gayle mistrusts the eager light in his eyes. Pities it, even. But later they will go to Peter's house—Lynn's house, really—and Gayle knows she will seek comfort where she can find it, and she will let him make love to her.

Peter has brought them all brownies: a peace offering, Gayle supposes, wrapped in cellophane and too big for one person, and yet he has bought three. Emme's is untouched; she has climbed into Peter's lap, something Gayle supposes hasn't happened in a very long time. But if he is surprised by this, or notices the tears drying on Emme's face, he doesn't let on. Gayle unwraps her dessert, intending to eat the whole thing. She will not look at Emme. She does not want to see the child's face, though she caught a glimpse before Emme buried it in Peter's shoulder. Its raw need.

Chewing stale brownie, Gayle thinks about what she should have said, back there in that dismal bathroom: how none of this will matter some day, and that Emme has more character in her little finger than all those girls put together. But the truth of the matter is that the ballet girls scare Gayle.

"I love you, Gayle," Peter mouths over his daughter's head.

Some people are just born losers. Gayle closes her eyes; she might stay with Peter—on some level they need each other, perhaps even deserve each other—but the thought of going through it all again with this unfortunate little girl, too unremarkable to be anything more than a burden to her own troubled parents, fills Gayle with despair. She understands what it means to be unwanted. But until now, it has never occurred to her that she herself might possess the cruel powers of denial.

"Are you going to eat your brownie?" she says. She stares at Peter, at the way he holds his daughter and strokes her head. Beneath Lynn's bed the ruined nightgown lay in silky pools. *Know your limits*, Gayle's father had counseled her once, on a rare afternoon they had spent together, fishing at the shallow green pond near the house—their home—with its brick facade.

"I'd hate for it to go to waste," Gayle whispers.

During the harvests, Emme's book had said, scores of birds were left broken and dying on the ground. What if even a handful had survived, roused into flight after the marauders were gone? What would have been enough to make a difference? Fifty? Five hundred? The hell of it was that nothing could make the difference, probably. Even birds must return to earth, to what lies in wait, and nothing was infinite: neither time, nor energy, nor love.

Phoenix

The housekeeper doesn't come on Fridays, so Orna has the morning alone. She can take as long as she likes, and so she stands before her round vanity table with the blinds closed against morning's pale slant. Two small lamps are burning on the table, casting their mellow glow. By this light she dresses, smoothing on her skirt and managing with some difficulty to fasten the tiny, delicate buttons of her blouse. She bends to see the clean meeting of skirt and blouse and thinks, reassured, that she looks all right. Just like the nurses said, and that was months ago, when she'd had to wear the thin, spotted hospital gown that gaped in back. God she'd hated that gown, but now she's in her own clothing again, a sensible wool suit of an expensive cut, and her figure is still fine. She shrugs awkwardly into the suit jacket and yearns for a cigarette—imagines herself chain-smoking, stamping out each butt in the green glass ashtray she used to keep here on the vanity. It's stowed, where now? August must have thrown it out.

She steps to the wall mirror and leans forward, studying the reflection. Her face is masked by the stretchy brown Jobst hood, which she wears almost all day, every day, to reduce scarring while her skin heals. It is close-fitting, like a ski mask, of a thick material that hugs the strange new contours of her face. Sometimes she imagines that the hood keeps her face together, packs tight the flesh and bone and coursing blood. Of course, she knows better—she has seen beneath the elastic and knows that the new skin is intact, a patchwork of mottled color that gleams like fluid, flowing up purplish-red to where her hair used to be. Nothing smooth, nothing right, but she is learning to focus on the details. Her right eye is still beautiful, a luminous green, and the other, although clouded and sightless, has the serene milkiness of an opal.

Orna is meeting her sister-in-law for lunch today. She had called Fredda earlier this week, her hands fluttering. "Lunch, Orna? Why that would be—*fine*," Fredda had said, her voice pleasant, if surprised. Fredda is an elegant woman, older than Orna by at least eight years, and Orna has not always felt at ease with her. But Orna has little family of her own left; her parents are gone, and her mother's sister moved to California when Orna was still a child. Orna has not eaten at a restaurant since the fire.

I will handle myself with assurance. With the silverware, I will be deft.

It helps that Fredda has seen her a handful of times since Orna's return from the hospital. Fredda has already asked the idiotic question, "Did it hurt?" and stared as though she could see through the hood to the face beneath. But Orna can forgive her sister-in-law this: she herself has spent hours gazing in the mirror, hood removed. What she feels is a curiosity at war with the horror. And the scars, by changing, allow her to chart a progress: early on, the tissue was pink, then red, then vascular purple.

When I walk into the restaurant my back will be straight as a dancer's.

Ready now, Orna goes to the full-length mirror on the inside of the closet door. She tilts her head at a calculated angle, turning so that she has a three-quarter view of her tailored suit and the sober brown hood. Somewhere beneath is the strange terrain of her face, the flap of ear which curves against her cheek like a shell.

—

She had been smoking in bed. Six months ago—a lifetime ago. August always hated that she did this, hated that she smoked at all, but Orna had been a smoker since age sixteen; it was nonnegotiable. For the first years of their marriage, August, thinking himself shrewd, would bring home pamphlets and books lurid with color photos: the lung before smoking, the soiled lung after—blackened, diminished. He'd leave them on the coffee table or in the bathroom, and Orna would make a show of leafing through them, pressing her face close to the pictures until the colors blurred together meaninglessly. She would reach out and tickle August, inducing him to laugh, pushing aside the lung pictures when they made love.

Finally, they reached an unspoken understanding: Orna would never smoke when he was in the room. Before sleep, she would suck meditatively on a cigarette, putting it out once her husband joined her in bed, fanning the air to clear the room of smoke. She would turn out the light, the nicotine still thrilling in her veins; she would wait for him to reach for her, and on many nights he did. He was still hungry, even after twenty-three years of marriage; *my love*, he would whisper, his hands wound in her hair, which had been dark and abundant.

But that night she had been tired, the cigarette loose in her hand as she read. She still remembers the way the smoke curled up lazily, beautiful even, in the light from the lamp by the bedside. Of the rest she remembers only parts, though August told her about it later, because she asked, his voice stunned and strange. How he had heard her screams and come running from his paneled study to find the bedclothes alive with fire and his wife writhing in the heart of it—her nightgown, filmy and light, and her lovely dark hair, in flames. How he had rolled her in a blanket to extinguish the blaze and called 911. She can remember a little of the ambulance ride, the crazy, keening siren and the lurching of the vehicle, but by then her eyes were swollen shut so tightly that the picture of August's anguished face, swaying like a moon over her when the ambulance skidded around corners, must certainly have arisen in her imagination.

—

The adult burn ward became as ordinary to her as her own living room: a wide, straight corridor, the entrance at one end, and at the opposite end the hydrotherapy room, sealed off by two sets of heavy doors. In-between was her room, plain and clean. She associates these familiar places with a hellish, indefinable pain. For nearly all of her burns were what they called full thickness, covering much of her left arm and extending to her hand and her head. The entire left side of her face required grafts, four in all, and a gauze packing was stitched into the side of her face so that the grafts would stay in place. For several days after the fire her face was so distended—eyelids squeezed shut as if sewn that way, her lips and tongue grown rubbery and huge—that she did not understand the one eye was beyond repair. Orna became hysterical and had to be sedated when she learned it could not be restored.

She had hydro every morning. Because of limited space, and the risk of infection, only one patient at a time was admitted to the tank room, a practice Orna despised. It meant she spent part of each morning waiting for her turn, listening for the sound of the cart coming down the hall to fetch her: a loose, disjointed clatter she learned to hate. By 10 a.m. the air in the tank room was so stuffy, so humid, and noisy—rock music pouring from the physical therapist's radio, the water pipes clanking. Her own screams. Bunched naked in the tank of warm water, she submitted to the therapist, who propelled her arms and legs in brisk apology. The nurses used small scrub pads to clean her wounds, and tweezers to pick at the dead, burned skin. Debridement, they called it, the word so perfectly clinical as to give no hint of the agony.

Because of the risk of infection, visitors were limited to immediate family, and everyone had to observe isolation procedures. At the entrance to the unit was a metal hamper filled with fresh gowns of a soft tan color; visitors were required to pull one over their street clothes before even entering the unit. August looked handsome in his flesh-colored gown. He came every night after work, and stayed until 8 p.m., when visitors were asked to leave. Required to leave, really, although sometimes the nurses let him stay later, pretended not to see him in Orna's room, for they liked him, and by extension, she thinks, they liked her, too.

"You're so lucky. He's a wonderful man," the red-headed girl on night shift said, her chin flapping with the start of what might be jowls. She meant to be kind, but Orna, dopey with medication, felt ashamed. After that she told August about the hydro in detail—and, later on, the God-awful itching that came as her wounds healed—so that he might appreciate and be proud of her strength.

But they did not talk about the smoking, or about the waxy ruin of her face, ever. "She's doing well, isn't she?" August would ask the nurses. He sat, straight-backed, in the molded plastic chair beside her bed, nodding and holding her good hand, though he always left the room when they changed the dressings. The nurses called to him when they were done and always he responded, looking from the nurses to Orna's good eye and back again, "You're saying that she's healing, right?" Dreamy with morphine, she held to August's hand and imagined the two of them floating up to the ceiling, out of the ward, lifted on the currents of air like ash.

—

The pain takes many forms and is hard to pin down: there is the raw cut where good skin was taken for grafts, the pitiless itching from the healing burns, and the pressure garments and splints— agents of her healing—which are thick and hot, relentless in their embrace. One night, after dreaming that she was in a medieval torture chamber, Orna awoke with a garbled scream, clawing at the tight brown elastic of her hood and reaching for August, even though he has slept in the guest room since the accident.

She dreads the reconstructive surgery that lies ahead—and when that is done, there is the question of cosmetic surgery. Her doctor, a placid man given to sincere-sounding pronouncements, advised her early on of the cosmetic procedures, telling her that they would have to wait until about a year after her injury, that the results would be an improvement. She knows not to expect to look the way she did before. To look beautiful.

On the nights when Orna has been crazy with pain and itching, she has thrown off the covers and lurched down the hall to the guest room. Standing in the doorway, she has told August that she will gladly accept any type of deformity if it means relief. He always shepherds her back to bed, clasps her good hand in his, talks in a calm voice: about work, their daughter Tandy, the book he is reading. Sometimes he says, "You're doing fine," and other times: "We'll do the cosmetic surgery, but that's not for a while yet."

She feels guilty after these nighttime breakdowns. The next morning she will study August carefully from across the breakfast table, strewn with his newspaper and the cups of coffee and high-fiber cereal he insists upon, for signs of disappointment or disgust. But always he kisses her gravely before leaving for work, perfectly attentive, and always Orna manages to smile at him, her face tight and strange beneath the hood.

—

They did not let her smoke in the hospital, of course, and so she gave it up, the discomfort of abstinence absorbed by the hell of her condition so that it was difficult to tell where one wretchedly began and the other ended. After returning home, she found she could take smoking, or leave it. She has not smoked since, except once, one indiscretion the morning Tandy returned to school in Madison. After the nurse had changed Orna's dressings and left her for the day.

Orna had stood at the window and watched the nurse's broad, white back receding down the walk. She was lonely in the house, restless but unwilling to go outside and risk frank stares. Before the accident she had run with a circle of women: middle-aged wives with whom she shopped and lunched and played tennis. The group had gathered two or three times a week, and although the women called after the fire, none came to the hospital, or visited her at home. Orna came to rely more and more on her daughter for company, although at first she had worried about Tandy, how the girl would respond to her ruined state. Their relationship was tentative, strained, at first; a sensitive child, Tandy acted falsely, loudly cheerful. Things improved when Tandy learned to help Orna at home, for August seemed reluctant. The nurse showed Tandy how to change the dressings, how to butter her mother with antibiotic cream before replacing the strips of gauze and helping her back into the elastic pressure garments, the splints on her hand and neck. After weeks of such intense scrutiny, such *intimacy* with her mother's changed face and arm, Tandy seemed to yield to a calm acceptance. These days she calls every day from school, a relief that she is far away just barely discernible.

The day Tandy returned to school, Orna felt her child's absence as pain. She wandered the house, waiting for her meds to kick in, a burglar in the hot, stretchy Jobst hood with holes for her eyes and mouth. She had passed the hall mirror, once, twice, forming a brown sketch in the glass: her facelessness more unnerving each time. Then she'd remembered the cigarettes in the pantry; minutes later, she was lighting up. The cigarette was only slightly stale, and she inhaled with relief, her identity once again fixed, right-seeming, in the rush of nicotine.

Something happened then: the phone rang, or the mailman sent bills clattering through the slot—she doesn't remember. But she knows that she extinguished her cigarette, frightened, stuffing the book of matches into the tattered sleeve of cellophane wrapped around the pack, jamming the whole mess into her winter purse, the black leather bag stowed neatly on a closet rack with the others. Where it remained, forgotten, or almost forgotten. Since then she has not smoked, although at times she imagines the taste of clear blue smoke, its fragility and bite.

She thinks about what it would mean to start smoking again. She teases herself with the sensuality of the act—considers the thin line that exists between smoking and not smoking and pulls back, shamed into piety. She will not smoke again—of course she won't—for what would that say to her husband, to her daughter? She so wants to please them—him—for not saying, *I told you so.*

—

A few weeks after Tandy returned to school, the nurse, Ida, had started to talk in earnest about teaching August to handle the dressings. She mentioned it to Orna more than once, then finally caught August after dinner one night.

"I think you should do it, sir." Ida moved around the kitchen, wide and slow, her voice sure. "I can show you—Tandy picked it up quick."

"Yes. The dressings." August had remained at the table, his hands flat against his thighs, and from his throat a clicking sound.

Orna stood abruptly, and the nurse's look swept from her to August, where it stayed, her face passing from annoyance to sorrow to pity.

"I'm sorry, sir. This is a bad time. Of course."

When Orna went upstairs soon afterwards, August's good night—"Sleep well, dearest"—had been even, if indistinct. But later that night she was awakened by a rhythmic, harsh sound. She climbed out of bed awkwardly, reaching for her robe and holding it close, following the sound down the hall, her feet rubbing soft on the carpet. When she understood that it came from August's study, she held her breath just outside the door, which was cracked open to admit a rod of stern yellow light. She had known without looking that her husband was weeping, having heard him cry exactly twice before in their married life: when his mercurial father died, and in the ambulance the night of the fire. Orna stood listening beside the door until her husband's sobs calmed, then stole down the hall to the bed that had become hers alone.

—

The next day, she heard the garage door open and close while she was still in bed, and when she ran to the front hallway, he was already gone. Orna stood in the light from the half-circle window over the door, still unwashed, and her face itching, itching, within the tight confines of the hood. She felt heated, unclean, and she paced in the bright hallway, trying to decide who to call—or if she should call August at work. A small brass clock on the table by the doorway read 7:30. She calculated swiftly in her head: if traffic were clear, he would be at his desk in twenty minutes.

She had called Fredda, his sister, instead. Fredda, with her cool, long face; in summer she wore sandals that exposed feet white as marble. A sour smell rose from Orna as she paged through the names in her little leather-bound address book.

She remembered something Fredda had said once at a family gathering before the accident, when Fredda's breath had been dry and sweet with wine. "Orna, I have a special place in my heart for my baby brother. I'm *so* proud of him but I'm proud of you, too, dear; you're almost like a sister to me. I want you to know that. My love is, is *impartial.*" The words so slurred and heady until August came to where they stood and Fredda fell silent, simpering.

Orna had dialed, telling the housekeeper who answered that she'd like to talk to Miz Fredda please; no, it wasn't an emergency exactly—more of a celebration, that's right, a *celebration*, for wasn't her sister-in-law drawn to happy things like a crow to what was bright?

And when Fredda answered in her laconic way that was caring, if you knew her as Orna did, Orna, in a voice with almost no quaver, asked, "Can we go to lunch, Fredda? Just us two? Let's get together, you and me."

———

When Orna steps out of the cab in front of the hotel, a small child looks at her, then gasps, his mother shuttling him away with a worried, apologetic glance. It is still early, and because she is afraid, Orna goes to an empty banquet room, instead of into the restaurant. She stands quietly amidst the vacant tables, hands to hood, breathing rapidly.

Orna waits until she thinks it is time, and then longer. When she finally walks into the restaurant, her head pressed low in its brown hood, Fredda is already seated. Silence falls when she passes the tables; some diners pointedly look away, but others stare. It is with some relief that Orna reaches the table where Fredda waits, toying with a glass of mineral water and smiling blankly. Fredda is a small woman with a sagging, expertly made-up face. As always, she is dressed expensively, today in a girlishly pink Chanel suit buttoned to her throat. Heavy gold bracelets cluster around her thin wrists, and they make a moneyed sound when Fredda stands to give her sister-in-law a stiff hug.

"Orna, *Orna*, sit down, dear. I can't tell you how nice it is to see you up and out. Good for you!"

Orna removes her coat and slides into her side of the booth carefully: no, *glides*, because she wants Fredda to see how well she is, how graceful and unchanged, even as she fusses with her purse and fans the linen napkin over her lap. When she glances up at her sister-in-law, Fredda is watching her attentively, and Orna allows herself to feel hopeful: that August's love for her is unchanged and that Fredda will tell her so.

"*Well*, dear, I can't tell you how surprised and pleased I was that you called," Fredda begins, with a smile that shows her teeth, surprisingly snub and beige for a woman of her means. "Tip and I have been in Phoenix, you know, but I've been keeping track of you through August, of course, don't think I haven't; and I must say, August worries about you all cooped up at home, and Tip and I do, too. I was so delighted when you suggested lunch. I said to Tip, 'Now *this* is a good sign.'"

Pleased, Orna says, "I'm feeling good." A waiter comes to the table, so smoothly as to almost seem to be on wheels. Even though his eyes flicker just a little when he sees her hood, still he is courteous and respectful, taking their orders quickly and smiling. Such a nice young man. Orna watches him back expertly away, feeling nervy, suddenly excited. She'd love to have a cigarette, but she did order coffee, and that ought to help; it will be good to have something in her hands.

"Well now, where were we?" Fredda says.

"Fredda, I'd like to talk to you about August," Orna says, shifting in the padded booth. "I'm worried about him. He's not quite himself lately—I don't think it's money, the medical bills, but he's been working so much and in the last couple of days I've hardly seen him." Poise has never been Orna's strong suit, and she realizes immediately that she shouldn't have brought up money, one never mentions money, but she continues, her hands suddenly damp and twisting under the table.

The waiter returns then, and there is an awkward silence as he arranges the cups of coffee and brings the tiny pewter pitcher of cream. Orna keeps her head lowered. When he moves away she looks up and sees Fredda's face, its odd, hard sheen.

"Are you asking me if my brother is upset, Orna?" Fredda chuckles, but the laugh lacks warmth.

Orna is flustered. She drops her spoon, retrieves it, her voice quaking, but just imperceptibly. "I wanted to make sure he was all right, that we're all right. We're all right, I think. Don't you?" There is the spoon, dropped again, and Orna ducking her head and saying in what she means to be a casual tone: "Don't you think so?"

"What do I think?" Fredda's smile is impersonal, and when she leans forward her bracelets make a dull sound. "What do I think? My dear, I find it hard to fathom you need to ask if something is wrong with my brother, but since you do—"

Orna reaches for her coffee nervously, spilling some on the table's white linen and wishing for the waiter to return.

Fredda cocks her head. "A man's wife is severely burned. She has several difficult—*episodes*—upon her return home. Well!" Fredda sniffs and leans even closer, lowering her voice. "Orna. Orna! He tells me that you don't want cosmetic surgery." Fredda leans back. The skin around her eyes twitches slightly.

Orna reaches up to touch her hood. "I need the reconstructive surgery. Cosmetic surgery is an option, but my doctor has been honest with me about what to expect." She grasps her cup in both hands, seeing suddenly that the coffee is milky like her eye. When Fredda doesn't respond Orna presses on. "I don't think it will be worth it. The pain. I don't think . . ." She looks around the dining room, its fleshy pink splendor. "I don't think it's necessary."

She stops. The waiter has returned, carrying a tray of food. He slips plates in front of each woman. "Anything else, ladies?" He is obsequious, Orna thinks, shaking her head, afraid to trust her voice; Fredda waves him off impatiently. "Yes, we're fine, thank you." Perhaps he wanted to linger; perhaps he wanted to hear what came next. Fredda inspects her butter knife, smiling without interest at her reflection in the narrow silver. "You've spoken with your doctor about this?"

Orna plunges a fork into her salad, lifts it to her mouth, then lays it back on the plate. Flowers ring the china; cornflower blue. "This isn't something to be entered into lightly, Fredda. The surgeries are incredibly painful."

"Yes. Well, I can appreciate that." Fredda looks appraisingly at Orna. "I think it's time to recognize that there are others besides yourself to consider." Orna's medication is wearing off and a raw, dull throb has set in. "I don't want you to think I'm unkind," Fredda says. "Of course I care about you both, but I do know that my brother thinks only of you, of the hardships you'll have to face if you don't go through with the surgeries. Do you really think you have the right perspective to make this kind of decision?"

The woman at the table beside them is red and round, her blouse as yellow as taffy. She frowns at her meal, at her blocky companion. It is clear she is in command; it is clear she is as rich as sin. "I understand," Fredda says delicately, sweetly. "I understand you were smoking in bed."

A moment passes. "I was," Orna says. The taffy woman gives a barking laugh, and then Orna says, her voice thick and hesitant: "Even if I had the surgery, it wouldn't be for several months."

"Well, then. Good. *Good!*" It is the voice Fredda uses for her inferiors: her housekeeper, her retriever, her drug-addled son. "Why make the decision right now?" Fredda is almost jolly. "Lord, dear, I haven't even seen your face. But August is my baby brother, and I can—well, I can only imagine! Orna. *Orna.* You are like a sister to me. I just want what's best for everyone, and I happen to know a little bit about cosmetic surgery. Oh, goodness dear, not *me!*" Her titter is almost a shriek. "I've got good genes, but several of my friends, they've had occasion to go to a Dr. Stan; I have his number right here, why not think about it, or at least not rule it out?" The hood obscures Orna's face but her good hand, reaching for the coffee, falls to the table limp. Fredda says briskly, "Now dear, let's face it, you need it."

Orna cannot bring herself to look at her sister-in-law. She stares at her ragged salad, hating herself for not understanding sooner that August and his sister have been talking. That they have always talked.

"I need it?" Orna's voice is loud, it must be, because the diners near them stop talking and look. "*I need it?* Goddamn you to hell," she breathes, touching her hood. Fredda's face catches between triumph and shock, and Orna sees the fine lines around her eyes, under the careful makeup. "If you'll excuse me," Orna says, securing her purse and pushing out of the booth. Past Yellow Taffy, threading her way between the close-packed tables. It is not until she has pushed the ladies' room door shut behind her that she allows herself to relax, braced against the door, all her muscles, even her bladder, unclenching, so that she wets herself. Humiliated she looks around, at ruffled curtains and shell-shaped soaps, a tiny gilt room. In the peach half-light she thinks of what is left of her face beneath the hood—rough terrain, mortar sluiced thick—and hugs herself. She pictures her coat, which still hangs next to the booth, but suddenly Orna doesn't care. She slips out of the ladies' room, heading for the front of the restaurant. She moves quickly and deliberately, careful not to look in the direction of the booth, which is on the far side of the restaurant, under the windows. A part of her is childishly delighted that Fredda will have to pick up the bill, and when she gets out to the hotel lobby she breaks into a skip, a run.

—

Wicked, wicked Orna. Outside the hotel she realizes that she doesn't want to go home. Not right away. So she hails a cab and directs the driver to go up Michigan Avenue, north through the park and along snaky Cannon Drive. She and August used to live near here before moving to the suburbs, and she tells the cabby this, an older man with the most splendid head of red hair. She loves his hair, but perhaps what she really loves is how he does not look back; if he sees her hood he does not react. They drive past the farm-in-the-zoo and up to the conservatory, a glassy, humid confection where she once went to a chrysanthemum show, gripping August's hand and exclaiming at the heavy-scented blooms. God, she was so young, then. The traffic crawls, but she doesn't mind. Everything looks familiar and yet not quite: rollerbladers dart among the bicyclists and joggers, and this stretch where she and August would walk on Saturdays seems smaller than it did when they lived here.

At Fullerton she tells the driver to cut west to the Kennedy Expressway. "Okay," she says. "Okay. Lake Forest, please." The cab surges through the light, and Orna catches her breath in an effort not to sob. A paper air freshener swings from the rearview mirror, filling the car with acrid pine, so that Orna cranks the window open. They inch down Fullerton, past neat brownstones and beneath the roaring el. The air smells of oil and dry leaves; a fine city grit pats her hood.

At DePaul University the driver jockeys for a clear lane, and the cab swings close to a young couple, brown-legged and sturdy, arms entwined. They are smiling, dreamy, their backpacks rucked high, and Orna can remember for a moment their perspective. In the days of their courtship, she and August would walk for hours, talking ardently, and when her girlfriends would complain of a boyfriend's or a husband's wandering eye, Orna felt secure: her own August's love for her inviolate. Orna sees how the girl dips her head shyly as the cab rocks past, and she suddenly misses August, a feeling that persists so that by the time the taxi pulls into her own driveway, she is eager to see him, and hopeful. It's past four and August's silver BMW is in the open garage.

He greets her at the door, his face stark. "Jesus, Orna, where have you been? Fredda called me in a panic."

For a moment Orna loses her momentum; she stands on the

front step, fearing the whiteness around his eyes. But there is the scar on her husband's brow—so familiar that she is comforted—and she steps forward and hugs August with her good arm. "I'm home now," she says, and allows him to lead her into the living room. When he offers her a drink, his words jitter and slur, and Orna understands that he has started without her.

"No," she says, but her husband, busy at the bar, does not seem to hear. When he returns to the couch, he carries two glasses of bourbon. He presses one into Orna's hand, and drinks his own in a quick, nervous gulp, his wrist snapping back precisely.

Orna's glass is sweating with cold. She puts it on the coffee table, where it is certain to leave a ring. "August," she says.

He sits down, leaning forward. The last of the day's sun is filtering in, highlighting his softening jaw line and silver hair. "Yes dear, tell me about it."

"I've been thinking about trust."

There is a pause as he regards her. "That's fine, Orna. Orna, that's just fine." He stands to pour himself another drink, and she sees that under his arms dark rings are forming. "You've had a long day," he says. He sloshes more bourbon into his glass, downs it immediately, then moves painstakingly across the living room to sit in the chair opposite her.

Orna stares past her husband to the picture window opening onto the back yard. The yard is long and green, its halfway point marked by a wooden gazebo that August built when Tandy was a little girl. It is the only thing August has ever made with his hands, and it makes Orna sad: no one has used the thing for years. The latticework flows up smoothly and ends in jagged peaks, like flames. "August," she says. "I want to know what you think of me."

"What I think of you," he repeats slowly, his voice so confused that she feels a stab of pity. "I love you," he says, then stands and shambles unsteadily back to the bar.

"Are you afraid of what I might look like?" She fumbles at her hood, then she's easing it off, pulling at the dressings. August's back is still turned, and she's not sure he can hear her over the rattling of the ice. "I want you to see me," she says, and that's when August turns; the hood and soiled dressings are in her hands, and August gapes, managing to say, "I love you, Orna." But she's watching his eyes, which are suddenly dull and hopeless, and she sees herself as he must see her, the webbed grafting and the colors—the purpled skin stretched tight and gleaming. That's when she knows that the surgery doesn't matter, not really—that it's not enough. Nothing will ever be enough.

"You were a beautiful woman," he says, and they stare at each other for a long, frightened moment.

She walks out of the living room then, moving straight to the hall closet, where she lifts her winter purse from the metal rack inside. She turns. August is in the living room doorway and he makes as if to come to her, his head rocking back and forth in apology, but she holds out the flat of her hand. *No.* Clutching her purse, she walks through the kitchen and out the back door.

Outside it is chill, dusky. Orna moves into the yard, her face held up to the air, which is spanking wet but not unpleasant. With deliberation, she paces out the twenty yards to the gazebo, her high heels sinking into the lawn. The gazebo was white once, but its paint is peeling now and the entire structure leans beneath a scum of dry vine. Orna sets her purse down on the bench inside, and because she feels that August is still watching her, she digs in it purposefully. Her fingers brush a tube of lipstick, a comb, a wad of Kleenex. And then she feels the edge of a pack of cigarettes, the illicit pack she smoked that one time, filched from the pantry what was it? Months ago? Years ago?

She pulls out the pack in its sorry sleeve of cellophane. The frayed book of matches is tucked inside. Almost without thinking she lights a cigarette and inhales, her eyes watering from sheer pleasure, flicking the still-lit match onto the floor. The flame extinguishes in the match's downward arc with a hiss. Orna looks to the living room window, where August stands watching her. When he sees the cigarette, he turns away.

All right then, she thinks, and with the cigarette clamped in her teeth, she lights another match and holds it aloft, close to a tendril of hanging vine, a dry spiral which accepts the flame with a puff like a tiny explosion. A whoosh, then a lick of orange; she lights another match and holds it against the skin of dry leaves on the bench; then another. Another!

The fire grows in seconds. Orna hears a tapping and looks through the vines, which shine like fiery wires, to the living room window. August is rapping the glass furiously, pointing at her. *Get away*, he seems to mouth, although in her current state she thinks perhaps he says instead, *Wet baby! Wet baby!* "Hee!" she manages, the laugh gurgling in her throat like vomit. *For Godsake get away.* August's face moves in and out of a shifting gold sheet, contorting in revulsion, or fear, she can't tell which. The wind shifts and the flames around her explode with crisp pops; what's left of the paint on the latticework is starting to blister and bubble with the heat. When she looks back at the window, August is gone.

The gazebo roof is a cap of flame; Orna is certain she can feel heat against the dead flesh of her face, and it thrills her. She understands that fire is constant, that it burns things pure so that the truth can be known. The back door slams and here August comes weaving, drunken and afraid. He runs to the gazebo and stands just beyond the blaze, flapping his arms and screaming her name. She can see him through the flames, lurching from side to side so comically that she laughs again and sinks to the wooden floor. When she tilts her head back, it seems to Orna that the flames rise into the air until the sky itself is blotted out, and the wood and dry leaf, blasted to cinder, ascend in the breathless heat until they can be dispersed by the wind, carried in pieces far away.

"Orna! Orna!"

Intent on the fire, she does not see how the gazebo is collapsing over and around her. Not until a chunk of roof, flaming, falls and strikes her shoulder, does she flinch and look to the place in the yard where August dances—duty-bound, she understands—behind the circle of fire. His arms swing in wide arcs. She waves back—all is forgiven—then gives herself over to the crazy, gorgeous blaze, the flames red and yellow, heated, she is certain, with the fury of love.

Darkness Can Fall Without Warning

The trip from Chicago to Paris takes seven hours, and Audrey is pleased at the prospect of meals on a tray, and the in-flight movie, a foolish romance that doesn't require thought. She adjusts the headphones so they fit snugly, and arranges on her tray table the things she has brought for the flight: a Russian novel, which she probably will not read; a trashy celebrity magazine, which she probably will; and herbal jetlag tablets that taste the way she thinks roses must. When she saw the tablets at the airport's travel store, she bought them, with a startled, appreciative joy, because that's what she would have done before she lost the baby. That's the way she is, or always has been: spontaneous, delighted. This is what her friends love in her. She is going to Felicia's to recover, as far away from home as possible.

From the airplane, she can see the frozen dogwoods and barren fields drop away. Finally she is escaping the burden of pity and reassurance—"You can always have another"—usually from women with three children, four; women whose pregnancies came as happy or not-so-happy accidents. It was winter when they lost their child, and it is winter still. The plane's narrow windows reveal a sky dusky as dry ice, and clouds ride below her, brittle and metallic. *It will be a relief,* she thinks, *to be in a place where no one knows.* Back at home, the farmhouse she and her husband Gideon are slowly, painstakingly, restoring is susceptible to drafts; at night Audrey clutches Gid beneath a weight of blankets. "This would have been a stupid house to raise a child in, anyway," she has said, her face buried in Gideon's neck, because night is the worst time: the pain she has kept in check all day cuts loose in staccato, corrosive bursts. The baby died before it knew more than the dim, warm recesses of Audrey's body. Audrey had thought it safe within the fortress of her bones. They would have named it Honor. Or William, if a boy.

The letter from Felicia came weeks before the miscarriage, on blue paper as textured and soft as the skin of a snake. Felicia, Audrey's friend from college, lives in Paris. Audrey saw this from the return address, and it was news; she hadn't heard from her friend in almost a year. *Come see me,* the letter said. *You and Gid, come see me,* the request posed with the artlessness of the very wealthy: it must not occur to her that others might be bound by schedules, jobs, budgets.

When she got the letter Audrey didn't take the invitation seriously, but less than a week after the D&C, Gideon brought it up over dinner. "Listen," he said. "We could swing one ticket. Why don't you visit Felicia?"

She and Gideon have been together seven years, and at first, Audrey didn't want to leave him for this trip. "Absolutely not," she said. But Gideon knows her better than anyone. Sometimes, Audrey thinks he knows her better than she knows herself; she will ask him, "What am I like?" Genuinely curious, as if Gideon is her mirror. In the end, she trusted that he knew what would help her. Felicia, whom Gideon has never particularly liked, doesn't know about the miscarriage, and Audrey doesn't intend to tell her. Babies won't come up; Felicia has never been interested in children.

—

Felicia meets her at the airport, which is high-ceilinged, tinged with yellow from the electric lights so that it looks neither modern nor clean. She is the same: bold cheekbones, lean body, careless in a dress that glitters a shiny, synthetic green. There is a gap between her front teeth, which are discolored a uniform beige: probably the tea Felicia drinks, a wicked, dark stuff that comes in metal cans. Felicia hugs Audrey hard, then takes her suitcase and strides ahead to a cabstand. A few paces behind, Audrey can see men stopping to look at her friend.

The ride to the city is gray, the morning dimmed by light rain and Audrey's exhaustion. The tablets were a disappointment, powerless to shut out the chatter of the woman who sat beside her on the plane, prattling about Versailles. "The walls are covered in go-wold," the woman, a Southerner, said. Audrey, sliding back and forth across the slick seat of the cab, tries to tell Felicia the story and spin it for laughs. But Felicia seems distracted. Or maybe it's Audrey, too tired to tell it right.

"You've lost weight—a *lot* of weight," Felicia says appraisingly, and Audrey turns to find her friend staring at her. "How long has it been since I've seen you?"

"Too long!" The cab skids on the slick road and Audrey leans forward, arm stiffened to brace herself. The effort of reconnecting is already wearing on her. "It's great of you to host me. Gideon says hello."

Felicia tips her head, examining herself in the driver's mirror. "Uh-huh. Hi back."

They are traveling on what seems to be a highway, called A-1, into Paris, but they could be anywhere: Audrey sees industrial parks, a hotel as bare and comfortless as a concrete bunker. Audrey will spend seven days in Paris, in Montmartre, in Felicia's flat, and she hopes it won't all look this barren. Audrey does not speak French, nor does she read it. She has not traveled without Gideon since their wedding. In fact, she has traveled very little. The cab rocks and they talk about the neighborhood where Felicia lives, which is working-class, she explains. Her apartment is right across the street from a cemetery. "Degas is buried there," Felicia says, pronouncing the name with strange, harsh inflection and preening a little, as if the status of living next to Degas' grave gives her a little extra cachet. They agree that they must go to the Louvre together, first thing tomorrow. Audrey wants to see the Louvre, but hopes it won't be too expensive. Felicia has family money, and over the years has lived in places Audrey has only seen on maps: Europe, South America, the Middle East. The cab is smoky and Audrey grasps for something else to say.

"Tell me about your painting. Are you taking classes?"

Felicia brightens. "Nothing official. I have a friend who's helping me out. He's a real painter, but he says I have promise.

And I've been modeling for him." Felicia pulls her hair up into a ponytail, then lets it fall. "Nude, of course." She laughs. "When in Rome, you know?" She turns to look out the window and Audrey, suspended between jealousy and admiration, laughs too.

"Tell me about you." Felicia twists away from the window and favors Audrey with an indulgent grin. "How's Gid? You two still whacking away at that—what is it? A *farm*house?"

Audrey loves her small frame house. It is surrounded by suburbia, but she and Gideon are carefully restoring it to what it might have been when it sat proudly on its isolated tract of land. The spare room they painted green for the baby is still empty; they hadn't yet bought the crib when Audrey miscarried. "Gideon's great," Audrey says after a pause. "Hey, show me where we are." She rummages in her purse for a map and spreads it, crackling, across her knees.

They are in a neighborhood of small, winding streets, narrow shops and apartments lit against the somber day. When the cab pulls up to a graystone building on a corner, Felicia snaps open her purse and pays the driver. It's raining, now. The front of the building is scarred with graffiti—whorls of navy and red that might be French—and the door, set deep in its socket like an eye, is a battered black. Audrey clutches her suitcase and backs against the building, trying to stay dry. Across the street is a high, ragged stone wall—"The cemetery," Felicia says. Audrey can just see treetops, dark with rain.

Inside the building, the halls are carpeted with a velvety material into which paths have been worn. "Elevator's out," Felicia announces, and Audrey trails behind, panting, as they climb the four flights of steeply pitched stairs. The apartment itself is charming, tiny, the walls painted a reassuring yellow.

"Make yourself at home," Felicia says. Then, pointing to the futon, "You'll have to sleep there. It's not too private, but you know me." She nods to the single bedroom. "I need my space. Besides, when I invited you, I didn't really think you'd come."

Audrey blanches. "I'll be fine," she says.

"Do you need anything right now?"

"I—I need to let Gideon know I made it."

"Okay, the phone's here." Felicia waves toward an end table, its tiny surface crowded with the phone and a photo: Felicia again, pouting from the jet frame.

Because of the cost, Audrey and Gideon have agreed to talk on the phone only twice: once upon Audrey's arrival, and once before her return. In order to make a call one must stand in the living room, tethered by the short cord of the telephone.

"Dial 00 first, and don't worry about being on too long," Felicia says, heading into her bedroom. "My folks set me up with a call plan." The bedroom door shuts, not quite a slam.

Audrey, who doesn't want to take advantage, leans against the wall and looks out tall French windows at a gray sky. The instructions on her calling card are easy to follow, and a moment later, she hears Gideon's voice.

"Are you okay?" he says.

She's gripping the plastic card, fingering its sharp edges. "Felicia lives opposite a cemetery. I'm looking down on it. Over the wall." A fine drizzle sluices the panes, blurring the graves together so that, seen from above, they are a maze. "The graves have flowers on them. I think they're plastic."

"Oh," he says. "What else?"

Audrey sees a couple of kids—boys probably—sprinting to the cemetery exit. Sequins of water rooster tail behind their pounding heels; their legs, in dark pants, are as thin as matchsticks.

"Guess we won't be making a baby this week," she says.

"It's too early. We've got time."

"Right."

"Don't worry," he says. "We're going to have an awesome baby."

"Enough."

"You're going to be an amazing mother."

"Enough!" Beneath the fixed drift of rain, the cemetery boys pelt one another with sodden leaves. "I have to go."

"Audrey—" Gideon begins.

"Goodbye, love," she says.

Inside Felicia's bathroom, the harsh white light is unkind. *My roots are showing*, Audrey thinks. She stopped dyeing her hair when they tried to get pregnant; she hasn't bothered to tend to it since, and the henna rinse has gone brassy. She bows to the sink and splashes water on her face. It is only noon, and she is stupid with jetlag, but she has to stay up the entire day, so her body can adjust to the time zone.

When Audrey emerges, Felicia says, "Damn, I thought you'd died in there!" Audrey, relieved that it isn't obvious she's been crying, manages a smile. "Listen, I have to run out for a bit," Felicia says. She has changed into the briefest of skirts and a strange fuzzy jacket that just skims her hips. "That modeling gig I told you about. Plus—" Here she giggles, elegant fingers pressed to her mouth. "I forgot you were arriving today and told a friend I'd meet him and go paint. I figured you'd want to sleep, anyway. Right? Okay if I leave you to your own devices?"

"Sure," Audrey says. "Go do what you have to do."

"I'll be back in time for dinner."

Audrey holds her smile until the front door closes, then she drops onto the futon, hands loose between her knees. Suck it up, she tells herself. You don't need a babysitter. She thinks of a meditation exercise she tried once—make yourself light—then stands abruptly. She can unpack, that's what she'll do: in her old hard-shell suitcase, her sweaters are carefully folded. She lifts them out, stacking them next to the futon along with the flat package they protected: an album of pictures from school, her and Felicia, faces still full as peaches. Young. Audrey found the photos in a shoebox and glued them into the album as a thank-you gift. Not something Felicia would do for herself, God no, and so something she might appreciate all the more.

They met in a literary criticism class in college, where Audrey was drawn to Felicia's easy glamour. "You're like the wife of Bath," Audrey told her friend once, hiding her jealousy. She envied the tangle of dark hair that just touched Felicia's shoulders, and the way she would sprawl in a chair, legs carelessly apart, like a man. Audrey was surprised and gratified when Felicia pursued a friendship with her: it turned out that Audrey could make her laugh—Audrey's imitations of their classmates, who tended toward pompous writerly types, were dead-on—and Audrey endured with amiable self-deprecation the mockery that Felicia occasionally turned upon her. They both loved movies. The theater on the deserted main drag of their college town showed matinees at 11 a.m., and they'd skip class to go, slinking into the dark theater with its spirit smell of mold and popcorn oil, its tired plush seats. The films were second-run, featuring orangutans and also Clint Eastwood, who had a way of holding his face still that Audrey has recently remembered and tried to emulate. After the film they'd emerge into the gray half-light of a winter afternoon, leaving their coats open, flapping, and walk, heads down, through the lowering day to a café. They ate what they wanted then—donut sundaes, or fries tapered and wet from the fryer—lingering until the waitresses started pointedly wiping down the empty tables around them, and refilling the ketchup bottles. They weren't eager to return to their dorm, which they described to each other as stifling, populated with "asses," Felicia said, and Audrey laughed at that, although she found the other girls subtly frightening. They were all rich, as Felicia was. Insular. Audrey, in school thanks to scholarship, was certain she was perceived as a drone, if she was noticed at all; she worked at her grades because she had to, and because, before Felicia, there was little else to do. Felicia could have gotten on well with the other girls, who courted her, but simply chose not to, and that was characteristic of her, Audrey learned, a perversity that Audrey thought of as integrity. Loyalty, even. But Audrey hardly expected that they would still be in touch, all these years later. She strokes the album with a fingertip, the glossy photo on its cover a close-up of her and Felicia, dressed in matching citron-colored shirts that Felicia chose for them that first month of their friendship, and paid for. The color suits Felicia's pale, luminous skin, and Audrey has picked it up in the yarn with which she bound the album.

Felicia has only lived in the Paris apartment for a few months, and perhaps because of this it has an impermanent look, Felicia's things lying about in a predictable clutter but seeming just that—only clutter—not essential to the rooms themselves. In the kitchen, Audrey opens the refrigerator. Inside are a few pieces of mottled fruit, a bottle of milk, cheese. If Felicia wanted to, she could just pick up and leave.

A few people are born lucky, Audrey thinks. She drifts into the living room, which is dominated by a fake fireplace and a mantel banked with white candles. Audrey picks one up and turns it over, examining it, digging a thumbnail into the soft, pale wax.

When Audrey had her D&C, they knocked her out. This had been a relief but also a disappointment: she had imagined the procedure to be like childbirth, with escalating waves of pain and then the immediate release. She remembers thinking that this might be the closest she'll ever get to the experience of birth, this might be all there is. Her doctor, a brisk, wiry woman with no pretense of tenderness, was annoyed that Audrey had worn her glasses, but the nurse had taken pity on her and let her keep them on so that she could see. Audrey had wanted her senses sharp for as long as possible. "I'm sorry," she'd said, teeth clattering. Sorry not about the glasses but for the weight of blood that had soaked her gown, emptying over her knees, before she even got into surgery. She'd lost two pints of blood; she needed a transfusion. Cold, so cold, as she searched for the single right word to say to that nurse.

Outside the window, over the wall, the cemetery glistens with rain, the slabs individuated now, dark wings. Audrey wraps herself in a wooly afghan spread across the futon, falling asleep to the scratch and coo of pigeons just outside the window. She wakes to the sound of rattling. Felicia sits cross-legged on the floor beside her, going through a cigar box of jewelry, and she holds up a pair of earrings that twinkle like mirrors. "How about these? You like?"

"Felicia." Audrey sits up. Her neck burns from sleeping, bent, on the futon; she can feel a mat in her hair. "How was your . . . thing?"

"Lovely," Felicia says, holding the earrings to her cheek. "Willem—my friend? He gave me this get-up. Gave it to me!" Felicia shifts so Audrey can see the dress, a diaphanous thing with narrow straps like bits of leaf. "Have you eaten? I can, you know, get you something. I mean, I can try, but . . . there's a party tonight. Just a little get-together, you know? You want to come? The food'll be good. You can eat there and meet some of my friends."

"Oh!" Audrey flutters her hands. "A party." She wants to want to go to a party. She imagines confident, contemptuous women and men in black turtlenecks; they will know all about jazz, she thinks. "Felicia, I should stay in tonight. Get over my jetlag."

Felicia looks both disappointed and amused. "Jetlag. Right. You don't mind if I go ahead, do you?" She's already standing, pulling out a green beaded necklace and draping it across her throat. "I won't be late."

"You go," Audrey says. For a moment she gazes, admiring Felicia in her shining attire. "You look beautiful," she says honestly.

"Oh, well. It's just a dress." But Felicia is pleased, her mouth quirking thoughtfully. "Listen." She leans down suddenly, putting her hand on Audrey's shoulder. "We'll go to the Louvre tomorrow. We'll have fun; your vacation can start then, okay?"

"Okay," Audrey says.

"And you'll be all right? I think there's cheese in the fridge." Felicia is already moving away, toward the door, hand to her hair.

"Leave me the key—I'll go out if I feel hungry."

Within minutes, Felicia is gone. 8:30, and in her absence the apartment becomes suddenly silent, expectant. Audrey paces the rooms with a mix of restlessness and relief.

—

The next morning they take the Métro to the Louvre. It's better now, it is, though Audrey feels shy of her friend, who today wears a Chinese-patterned jacket and pants of a soft, billowy cut. Her sandals are paired with odd, thick socks. On the Métro, Felicia chews aspirin tablets with fierce concentration: "Hangover," she explains, which does not stop her from telling Audrey about the party, and the man she met. "A poet," she says in a conspiratorial whisper. "You know how *they* are."

"Sure." But saying this, Audrey feels lonely.

"Lots of drama," Felicia says. Then she crosses her arms over her chest and closes her eyes. It used to be different. They used to be on the same team, the way they could talk about anything: the purported affair between their pallid Spanish instructor and the handsome, if dissipated, classics professor; the anorexic girl on the floor below them who'd suddenly, unexpectedly, ballooned in weight. "She's pregnant," Felicia had said with malicious certainty. They made do with these scraps even as they pledged to each other that they would live life fully once they got out of school.

When they get to the museum, Felicia plops down on a bench. "Listen," she says. "I feel like shit. You go ahead; let me pull myself together here. Meet in two hours?"

"Two hours," Audrey agrees. Though she would have preferred to stay with Felicia, right by her side, she looks at the museum's brochure, uncertain about how to set off on her own. The museum's halls radiate in every direction and she wanders, clutching her map and passing unthinking through the galleries until she reaches the Mollien room. This place is deep red, murderous; the paintings—French, nineteenth-century—shimmer

with death. Here there is little dignity in endings. The dead lie
shoeless, or worse, half-shod: a twisted sock trails off a naked foot
on *The Raft of the Medusa*. Shipwreck, Audrey learns, staring at a
pale reproduction of the painting in her brochure. The placards
next to the paintings are in French, but the mute terrors of these
pictures—their blazing rooms and martyred women, drowned or
bleeding—do not elude her.

What if I'd died, she thinks, staring at a painting of an ethereal
woman, head limned with a halo. *During surgery, or childbirth.* In the
background of the picture, a dark figure approaches on a horse.
What if the baby had lived instead of me? Audrey imagines Gideon
caring for a newborn on his own, missing Audrey, of course, but
so taken up in his new and daunting responsibilities that he could
not recall the shape of her face. Audrey shakes her head. If she
had died, his life would go on.

She leaves the gallery quickly, in search of the café where she is
to meet Felicia. As she climbs a stone staircase, the steps scalloped
from use, four young adults trudge down past her with a baby
carriage held aloft between them. They are like pallbearers, their
faces set.

—

The museum café is crowded with Asians and Americans. Felicia
arrives minutes after Audrey, in the company of a security guard
with a soft, pocked face. The two of them are laughing. "Au
revoir," Felicia trills to the guard, grabbing Audrey's arm and
sweeping into the café. They order coffee at a counter; it is served
in tiny cups, with twists of paper filled with sugar. "That guy
wanted a date. Can you believe it?" Felicia links arms with Audrey

and for a moment it's like the old days: partners in crime.

When they secure a table, Felicia looks at her expectantly. "So? What did you see?"

The security guard has reappeared at the entrance to the café, looking plaintive. Audrey laughs uncertainly, trying to describe the time she spent in the red-room Mollien.

Felicia's smile is almost kind. "Always so *earnest.*"

"No, listen," Audrey says, her face burning. "There are so many ways to die. There are—there are more ways to die than there are to live." To avoid looking at the guard, who has edged into the café, Audrey turns and surveys the surrounding tables.

Next to them, a middle-aged American couple speak in loud voices and plot their conquest of the Louvre over the remains of two salads. "We've got to move faster," the woman complains.

"Most people don't really have choices," Audrey says. "We just think we do."

Felicia has taken a cigarette and propped it, unlit, in the corner of her mouth. "Welcome to the real world," she drawls.

"You understand, then," Audrey says. Relieved, she gulps her espresso. Since the miscarriage, Audrey has returned to caffeine with an angry relish. This coffee is strong and thick. The cup is small enough to cover with her hand.

"People *think* they have choices," Felicia says, waving her hand dismissively. "But the real stuff is mapped out for us."

Next to them, the American couple rises to leave. They're both overweight; the man's pants are held up by a belt made of slick brown vinyl.

"Take them, for instance." Felicia nods at the Americans, making a little moue of her lips. "They're fated to be fat. They may think they can go on a diet, but their destiny is already ordained. To eat like pigs!" She sniggers, crushing the unsmoked cigarette into her coffee cup and standing. "Mark my words, it's only a matter of time before they're chowing down on croissants."

"Their. Fat. Fate." Suddenly Audrey is laughing, too. She feels dark, exhilarated. Excitedly, she grabs Felicia's arm. "But what about the things that happen to us?" she says. "Like in the paintings?"

"Same thing. Fate. And the only way to deal with fate is to not pretend you have any say in the matter. Give in to it, and you won't be disappointed." Felicia stretches her arms high over her head so that her jacket hikes up, exposing the smooth cream planes of her belly. "Come on. Let's go. I'm sick of this place." She picks up her handbag. "Monsieur Lonelyhearts is gone, I think."

Audrey pushes away her cup and stands to follow her friend. "How did you meet that guy, anyway?"

"Who? The poet? Oh, the *guard*. I was sleeping on the bench. He came over to kick me out and I charmed him. Now he's a pest!"

Audrey thinks of Gideon; at night they play Scrabble, listen to music. They watch the same old movies, over and over again.

"*Come*," Felicia calls.

Audrey smoothes her hair and starts after her friend, who is well ahead of her, already weaving her way between the tables.

—

They take the Métro back to Felicia's neighborhood and stroll through the web of narrow streets. The dome of Sacré-Coeur looms above them as they leave canyons of narrow shops and enter the open sprawl of markets, with their great veined cabbages, tomatoes, flowers packed tightly into shoals of color. In a glass case, a chicken head lolls, scooped out, eyeless. Audrey reminds her friend of the walks they used to take in college—"We used to cut class; we didn't take everything so seriously"—and her voice trembles with emotion. "Who would have thought we'd end up in Paris!"

"Well, we've both changed, yes?" Felicia says. She's looking in a shop window at gem-colored sweaters.

"Changed?"

"I think I'd look good in the blue, don't you?" Felicia pushes into the shop without waiting for an answer, and Audrey, trailing behind, watches her friend buy three sweaters in quick succession, nodding vigorously when Felicia suggests it might be time for lunch.

Across the street is a small café screened with awnings; at a table by the window, they order soup and dessert. Felicia tells her more about last night's pseudo-Byronic poet. "He smelled," she says. "He thinks it's European not to bathe. But he's very soulful, and he seems smart." Then she flatters Audrey by asking, "What do you think? Should I call him?"

By the time the waiter returns with their lunches, Audrey feels overcome by a giddy recklessness. "Call him!" she almost shrieks, then lowers her voice when a woman at the next table, sunken cheeks aflame, glares. "Listen, I've been thinking," she begins.

"So what do you want to do this afternoon?" Felicia is already digging into her dessert, a complicated pastry with a chocolate lattice. "We can go to another museum. The Rodin is good." She cuts the pastry open and pokes at the yellow cream inside. "We could go to a market."

"Felicia," Audrey says. The pulse in her throat beats hard. "That thing about fate." Felicia, still sawing away at her dessert, looks up lazily. Audrey swallows. "I really believe that. I just wanted to say that it means a lot to me that—that you do, too. That you understand what I mean." She flutters her hands before dropping them into her lap.

"Great minds think alike," Felicia says. Licking her fingers, she winks at Audrey.

"I had a miscarriage," Audrey says. Outside the window, slim Parisians in black leather jackets rush by.

Felicia puts down her knife and gapes. "No shit," she says finally. "No shit."

Audrey's face warms, and she feels the way she used to in college when she made Felicia laugh: powerful, shy. She bows her head humbly, then lifts it. "Fate," she whispers.

"It gets us all eventually," Felicia says, and Audrey waits: for the elaboration, a revelation, that irrevocable thing that will connect them again.

At the door, an older man with a long, chapped face looks at them with recognition, then starts across the room. Felicia glances up and brightens. "*This'll* cheer you up. This guy is a hoot." Audrey stares at her friend, but then Felicia smiles at her in so beguiling a manner that Audrey, confused, smiles back.

The man wears a wool scarf and a neat tweed coat, everything about him clean and spare except for the botched nails, which Audrey notices when he stops at their table. They are chewed to the quick, rimmed with old, dark blood. He bows and says bonjour. He holds a brown hat, banded in red, at his waist. "I am Jean Paul," he says to Audrey, extending his hand. His English is hesitant but precise. "You are a friend of Miss Felicia's?"

Audrey nods. Felicia grins meaningfully at her.

"I have had the pleasure of seeing your friend in this café. She is—" Jean Paul looks to the ceiling, groping for words. "How do you say? Very kind. Very kind to listen to an old man."

"Jean Paul is a collector." Felicia smiles broadly. She gazes at him, assured as a cat.

"Yes, yes." Jean Paul fishes in his pocket for a handkerchief and dabs at the corner of his mouth. He has a striking head of white hair, magnificent as a lion's ruff. "Ornements de Nöel."

"Christmas ornaments," Felicia says.

"Yes. Ornaments. And it is my love for these ornaments that has made me—j'ai fait faillite."

"He went bankrupt," Felicia explains to Audrey.

Jean Paul furrows his brow and raises his hands, palms up, as if to show his own amazement at these developments.

"How interesting," Audrey says.

Jean Paul bows again. "Perhaps you and your friend would like to see the ornaments sometime?" He looks at Audrey, but the question is really addressed to Felicia.

"Audrey?" Felicia leans over the table toward her. Her lips are parted, greasy with soup. "How about today? How about now? What do you think?"

Audrey looks out the window. The low-slung day is giving way to intermittent brightness: light skittering hectic through patches of cloud. She is suddenly afraid she will start laughing, have to cram her fist against her mouth. She is in Paris! Her heart flutters.

"Why not?" she says, and Felicia, eyes sly and merry, claps like a child.

—

Jean Paul lives near Sacré-Coeur, in a neighborhood that was probably once charming but which is now overrun with tourists in tracksuits, wearing berets. Audrey knows without anyone telling her that she is to take her shoes off before entering Jean Paul's apartment. Inside, the foyer is bright, the gold-painted walls glittering as if covered with foil.

"Come see my beauties," he says, and inclines his magnificent head.

"Uh, how well do you know this guy?" Audrey whispers to Felicia as they proceed, single file, along the narrow passage.

"You're safer here than in my own living room," Felicia says sotto voce. "Just don't touch the Goddamn ornaments. I guarantee you he'll freak out."

"I didn't know you'd been here before," Audrey says. "Sorry."

"Something to do, eh?" But Felicia is already striding ahead, and she might not have said this, not in that way.

The bedroom is dark, papered in dull red fabric and lit only by the Christmas tree, which dominates one corner, its false branches brushing the wall and the dresser, the windowsill with its shell of smooth, cream enamel. Ornaments are clustered so thickly that it's hard to make out one from another: blinking, her eyes adjusting to the dimness, Audrey finally distinguishes what looks like a hanging basket fashioned from tinsel, and an angel, its foil body surmounted by a staring china head. Each looks fragile, polished to a dull gloss with age. Audrey and Felicia assemble like dutiful children before the tree, and Jean Paul launches into an explanation in French.

At first Audrey tries to look engaged, but because she cannot understand him, her eyes wander. Heavy red draperies frame the window; on the pristine dresser, a comb, brush, and mirror have been lined up meticulously. The bed is narrow as a nun's, with a tight, hard pillow roll centered at the head.

"He says he went bankrupt buying ornaments, and had to sell everything," Felicia says, poking her. "It took him five years to find these ornaments, to replace the ones he'd lost." Audrey nods, but Felicia pokes her again. "Listen up. He's talking to you. *You* haven't heard this story five million times!"

But he isn't talking to Audrey; Jean Paul's eyes are locked on Felicia, on her hair and her pale shoulders, as sharp as wings. Audrey can hardly meet her friend's sly gaze; something about the apartment has diminished her merriment. She nods again, swinging her eyes back to the angel ornament, which almost has a baby's face, captured in the glossy china like a fly in amber. "Every year I find myself putting the—the *beauties*—up earlier," Jean Paul says. He's speaking in his precise English again, finally looking at Audrey. "I miss them, you see."

Audrey pretends not to hear when Felicia snickers behind her. When Jean Paul beckons she follows, back down the narrow hallway and into the living room, where the walls are covered with coppery flocked paper, and there is another tree, funereal, bowed with its weight of waxen angels and paper-cut figures. Lacquered glass balls capture distorted images of the room in which they stand; there are double-faced Santa heads and cruel, faceted tin stars; one ornament features a child's head, dim as a blown candle and nestled in grapes. Audrey hates the tree.

"Tell us about this one," Felicia says, and Audrey, searching Jean Paul's face, sees in his pouched eyes a knowing despair.

Don't, she wants to cry. She puts out her hand, but Jean Paul, gazing at the tree, is already saying softly, "I am not where I thought I would be at this time in my life."

"Sir," Audrey says. Her hand hangs in the air between them. "It's okay." She means to be kind.

Jean Paul cocks his head, a sparrow's movement; he gazes at her and his eyes, in their purses of flesh, look bright. "To some people, these things come easily, yes?"

"Yes," Audrey whispers.

"But we know how it is, don't we?"

Audrey doesn't trust herself to speak. Almost nodding, she looks hard at his spotless lapel.

"This is my destiny," Jean Paul says simply, and with a swing of his arms indicates the room and the tree. "I accept it."

"Hell-*o*." Felicia bumps against her with a grunt. "Earth to Audrey."

Audrey turns. Felicia's face is just inches away, grinning contemptuously. The strong lines of her nose, her mobile and comical mouth, are still beautiful. She has always been beautiful, Audrey thinks: effortlessly, unthinkably beautiful.

"Looks like you two have hit it off," Felicia says. "Looks like you two have a lot in common." She laughs, a raw, low throttle.

"He's like us," Audrey says.

"The day he's like me I may as well kill myself," Felicia whispers. She's smiling.

"Well, *I* am like you, then," Audrey says. "I *am*." She hates the plaintive sound of her voice. She wishes she were different, and this wishing is like unearthing a childhood doll, or dress, something she might have imagined she'd outgrown. In college, Audrey used to dream of shocking Felicia with her daring. She would imagine herself doing things Felicia wouldn't expect— getting stoned, getting laid—and the surprised admiration Felicia would necessarily feel for her.

"Tell me about this one." Audrey reaches for one of the glossy balls. She can see her hand reflected in the dark, mirrored surface, the way the image grows larger until everything in the background is blotted out.

Jean Paul lets out a little shriek. "Please! No!" he cries, and Audrey snatches her hand back.

"I wasn't going to touch it!" she says.

Jean Paul looks as though he might weep. "The ornaments, they are fragile."

"I'm sorry," she says.

"Don't be sorry for me!" he snaps. Then, in a gentler voice, "I thought it was understood that you had to take care." Jean Paul shakes his head. He has stepped between Audrey and the tree. "I share my beauties with almost no one; I thought you would appreciate what I have done."

"I do!" Audrey backs up. "I do. I just wanted to know about that one. Its story."

Jean Paul pivots abruptly on his heel and that's when Felicia laughs outright, a ragged snorting, ill-concealed behind her hand. The man must think it's Audrey because when he turns around again he's talking to her, his voice high and thin. "And how could you understand? How could you, little girl?" He shakes his head again and again. "You are nothing like me."

"There you go," Felicia says. "You should have kept your hands to yourself."

Jean Paul's fists press the sides of his head. Audrey imagines the roaring he might hear: all that surging blood.

"Americans: so *privileged.*" Jean Paul sneers, and turns away. "Goodbye," he says to Felicia over his shoulder. He bends to the tree, straightening an angel with candy floss hair. "Goodbye!" he barks when they don't move, and that is what Audrey will try to forget later, the man bending to his paper angel, as if to a lover.

—

Outside, the weather has brightened. The sun brings into a clear, merciless relief the carts of vegetables, the pennants that crisscross the street and flap like laundry.

"Whew!" Felicia says. "I could use a drink after that. What a nut." Her voice is mocking, but then she falls silent, pursing her lips around a fresh cigarette.

"That was horrible," Audrey says. She can't bear to look at her friend. Across the street, a man in a jumpsuit swipes at water and rubbish, moving them along the gutter with the stiff green bristles of a plastic broom. *I'm in Paris*, she thinks, understanding that it doesn't matter where she is. "He thought that was me, laughing."

"*That* was pathetic," Felicia says.

"Oh, come on!" Audrey feels near tears. "I felt bad for him."

"Oh, yeah, so bad you had to paw his ornaments!" Audrey winces, but Felicia has started giggling. "Audrey, who cares what he thinks? He's a freak. A loser." She exhales a plume of smoke; her voice sounds bored. The man in the jumpsuit sweeps past them, his hands blunt, dark knobs on the broom.

Audrey imagines what Felicia will suggest next: some out-of-the-way bar and restaurant patronized by regulars whom Felicia will claim to know. They will go to this place, or somewhere like it, and there will be a woman at the bar sporting three teeth, wearing pajamas, and Felicia from her wicked, privileged perch will condescend to greet her like an old friend.

"I shouldn't have gone along," Audrey says. "I didn't have to."

She reaches for Felicia's cigarette, but Felicia feints, holding it just out of reach.

"Darling, don't ever lose your sense of humor. You're boring without it, don't you know?" She's giggling again, puffing on the cigarette and prancing. When Audrey doesn't say anything, Felicia stops and takes a serious drag. "I see. Feeling bad, are we?" Felicia flings her cigarette to the sidewalk, eyes narrowed. "You haven't by any chance found religion with your Gideon, have you?" She throws her head back, and in a mincing falsetto proclaims, "Oh, suburban God of my Fathers, deliver me from my sinful ways! I am a . . . a *sinnah!*" She shrieks with laughter, which tails off when Audrey doesn't join in. "Christ! You used to be fun. Oh, go have your babies! Face it. Your life is over."

"God damn you!" Audrey says. A woman across the street, gripping a net bag bulging with tomatoes, stares; her eyes meet Audrey's, then drop away. Chill certainty floods Audrey's chest so that suddenly she isn't angry anymore. When she turns to Felicia her voice is almost normal. "What do you see in me, anyway?" Audrey asks. "Why are we friends?" But she already knows the answer, and she understands that after this visit, she will probably never see Felicia again.

Felicia is, for just a moment, startled; her face takes on a soft, yielding look. Then she regains herself. "C'mon, I'm getting a drink! Forget all this and let's get trashed." She drapes her arm around Audrey's rigid shoulders; after a moment she lets it drop away, shrugging. "Suit yourself. Jesus. Do you know how to get back to the flat, at least?"

"Yes," Audrey says. Felicia is already walking away. "I know."

"Keys," Felicia says. She actually throws them, tossing them over her shoulder without looking back. But Audrey waits, watching Felicia move alone down the street, the stiff-legged saunter; only when her friend is out of sight does Audrey pick up the keys and take off in the direction of the flat. Her chest feels light, as though it is filled with something bubbly and pink. She unlocks the door and rushes to the phone, not bothering, this time, to use her calling card.

"Gideon!" she says. In a confused, agitated voice she starts to tell him about the Christmas ornaments. She means to explain how funny Jean Paul is in his natty hat, how the ornaments make her laugh and laugh, and he should be glad because finally something is funny, isn't it?—but the way it comes out is that the angel ornament has tiny wicked teeth, and the basket—God, the tinsel basket is a dull sleeve after all, filled with nothing.

She pauses, out of breath.

"Audrey, what's wrong?" Gideon's voice has ratcheted to alert, the way it did when she woke him to tell him about the bleeding. She imagines him sitting up in bed, the straight line of his back.

Audrey presses the phone against her ear. "Our baby," she finally breathes.

She used to imagine what their baby would look like: the dignified face, body smelling sharp and sweet as cider. Now, eyes closed, she leans forward as if into a gale. Audrey already understands that she will look back on this moment with the bittersweet satisfaction of nostalgia. She considers the long life she hopes she and Gideon will share

"I haven't given up," she says, and in her voice is the fear of all that might come. Willing Gideon to understand her narrow escape into faith, uncharted, Audrey opens her eyes. The sky is honeyed, blurred with light. But now, she knows that darkness can fall without warning.

Repo Man

'll call him Glenn. He was a repo man and he claimed he liked the hours. "I can set my own clock," he used to brag, though that wasn't exactly true: he was at the mercy of his clients, really; you got to get to them when they're home. So you roll in early, or late, however you look at it. Glenn used to climb out of bed at 3, 4 a.m., depending on how far he had to drive. He had a big territory, fifty miles in any direction. He had respect within his field.

He wasn't supposed to be doing this. He'd gone to school. For almost two years he studied at Mineral Area College, and if he didn't get his associate's, how close was he? Maybe a semester or two short, it was hard for him to say. He meant to go back once he made up some debt. He took that first job just for the money, a chop shop south of Chicago, but then Carly and him, they hooked up and had the boy and—blah blah blah, haven't you heard all this before? Same old story with the sad sack waking up just this side of forty. He'd never claimed to be unique.

He understood his clients. He called them clients, sure. He knew what it meant to want a car, a certain car, how it could tell on a man. His life could be in the shitter but he always had a good ride. People who lived cars made judgments: the seats had to be leather, and power was everything; he told me he cried the day they stopped cranking out V-8's. God's Glory: you want what you want. He knew something about that.

You need a partner when you repo, and in the early days he had Carly. "She waited in the car," Glenn used to tell me. "Not like you." A second pair of hands: you got to have 'em because what if you get there to collect and things go the way they should and the car is where it should be? You take it, however you can, and then you need a second driver to bring your own car back. Some used tow trucks, but that was never Glenn's style; too flashy, he said. He wore his hair cut flat and short and those loud, bright shirts, printed with palms and pineapples, girls with apple breasts doing the hula. His jeans were pressed. Once he showed me a book from his college days: *Dress for Success*—and that's how he styled himself, always his own way. He wasn't a man to take cues from others, Glenn.

We got close the year he split from Carly. I met him in Tracy's, a dive bar west of Chicago. He didn't have a partner anymore, and I was out of work, my luck thin. I'd tried college, but it didn't take. I'll be straight with you: I was down on myself then, weepy and weak-willed. When my dad called me lazy, or maybe he said loser, I believed him. I needed to be reminded that I had my talents. Gifts, Glenn called them. *Astor*, he would say, *we need to focus on your gifts*. I was his project, I guess I can see that now, and so far as I was concerned he was a college man. When he started sleeping with me I told myself I wouldn't do this well again, never.

I've had my share of boys pretending to be men—college kids; entitled, mean—and older men who looked good at first, but when they came close you could see life had made them hard. Glenn was different. He had a way of putting things. I have slept, I am here to tell you, with a learned man.

We met in July and moved in together August 15, a little apartment in the King Arthur Courts. By mid-November, we had a routine: bed early, coffee at 3 a.m., then hit the road by 3:30 to catch the first client. It was dark when we woke, dark when we drove. Glenn worked for three different repo companies; they faxed him the orders, and some days were full, but on others the job would be done by breakfast, and we'd celebrate over eggs and black bacon. We knew all the greasy spoons west of Itasca, where we'd order our $3.99 specials and the bottomless cups and drink coffee until our teeth ached. Then it was home for sex, and bed, because the job started all over again the next morning. It was a good life.

"Astor," Glenn would say in the quiet of our room. "Astor, *you* are a natural." He liked that I didn't go sentimental when the clients bitched or cried; I stood my ground. I never hounded him like Carly did, back in the bad old days, over the single mothers, the grandmas with their Bonnevilles so rusty the side panels looked like lace. "You have heart," he said, kneading my naked breasts, then taking a hit of Jim Beam, "but not too much. I don't have to worry about you." My folks had divorced with the usual fireworks: I guess Glenn liked the sound of that, he thought it had made me tough and capable. "You're a woman can stand on her own," he said, and I didn't tell him otherwise, because when I was with him I thought it might be true.

We had a full slate that day in November, three stops, one of them so far west of Chicago I joked to Glenn that we would see the fucking Rockies from the guy's back porch. We hit that job first, planning to work our way back, but we got out there so early we had to sit and wait for the first gray light of morning. The client's name was Revere, and he lived in a tract house that had seen better days. We drove past and parked a few houses down, our lights off. The neighborhood wasn't bad, most of his neighbors gave a damn, but Revere's window had an American flag curtaining the front bay, and toys littered the yard though frost had hardened the ground.

When we waited like this, Glenn liked to tell me about runs he'd been on: "Danger nights," he called them, perfectly serious. The man was proud. There was the time cops pulled him over because the client's daughter had called 911 when Glenn hot-wired the car. "I had to talk myself out of *that* one," Glenn said, laughing. Sometimes clients tried to stay a step ahead of him, moving from home to work, parking the car at a neighbor's or sister's, but Glenn knew how to track someone down. "I'm like a federal agent," he would say. "People don't see it, but I am Magnum fucking P.I." Always in the stories it was us versus them, Glenn battling the asshats, he called them, and I know he meant for me to understand that I was part of his team. Why else would he tell me about the women he met on the job, making me laugh when he imitated their piping little voices so that I could almost see the candy fluff of their hair. "'My husband, he doesn't know I haven't been keeping up with the payments,'" Glenn would squeak. "As if I wasn't a professional! Raddled, she was. Blowsy." He used words that I had to look up afterwards; I admitted this to him once, without telling him how often it happened.

The lights were still off at Revere's, so Glenn passed me a

cigarette, lighting it with his own. "When I was a young man, I thought I was destined for big things." He inhaled and looked straight ahead down the dark street. "Big things," Glenn repeated. "I thought I was special." He laughed then, without satisfaction. "Then I found out how hard it is, how *lucky* it is, just to be average, that that alone is an accomplishment in this world. You see what I've seen—" He got genuinely thoughtful; the man could be deep. "I been strangled by crackheads. You tell me it ain't something to just be normal."

"I hear you," I said, though Glenn was anything but average. I saw something in him, a brilliance, or intensity, that attracted and frightened me both.

"I make a living and I take good care of my kid. I've been lucky," Glenn said, and meaning it, I agreed that he was lucky.

That morning all he really wanted to talk about was his son. "It's a Camaro," Glenn started off, because he began all his important conversations with cars. "This guy is serious. You look at that car: no pussy automatic in that baby, and he got the SS. Uh-huh." Glenn grunted approvingly when I nodded; I knew by then what the SS meant: 340 horsepower. A V-8. He stabbed a finger at the house. "This one got in over his head; I'll bet he spent 10, 15K on the SS alone. That's one thing about my boy, Sam," he said, and just the way he tended to say the name, all low and calm, told me how he felt about that kid. "Best thing I've done. He reminds me what's what." Glenn should have been in a good mood—talking about Sam usually did that to him—but instead he was jumpy and irritable, chewing at his lip while we watched the house. Carly and him, they had their differences, usually involving the kid, or money, and I wondered if more trouble was coming. The boy was supposed to stay over later in the month, for Thanksgiving, and Carly sometimes made claims: how Glenn had a temper and she worried about her child. "*Her* child," Glenn would say, genuine hurt in his voice. "I would *never* hurt my son." He used to be a drinker; hell, he'd done it all, shooting up, losing time, then going cold turkey when he realized Carly was serious about keeping Sam away from him. "I can understand how it was then," Glenn said. "I respect that. But I'm okay now. *That* was when I had a temper."

I said something then, the way I did, to encourage him. "The thing about this business is that we're doing a service," he continued, almost as if I hadn't spoken. "People—*some* people—" he said, "need a kick in the ass. And I speak respectfully, having been there myself. They need to be told to stop pissing it away." He straightened in his seat, his neck rattling. "It's up to them after that." I rubbed Glenn's back and told him I understood. "Me?" Glenn said. "I've been clean four years now. What do you think of that?"

"I think it's cool," I said, and set to work, rolling more cigarettes for us both. I'd given up pot when I moved in with Glenn, but I still liked hand-rolled tobacco. My cigarettes are tight and lean. "You're a good influence on me."

"Yeah I am," he said, but he didn't smile, so I set in to talking about things we might do together, him and Sam and me. I can't say I have a jones for kids, the way some women seem to, but I liked this one fine. Who wouldn't love Sam? He's a nice boy, smart like his Daddy, big eyes bright as sequins. He was six then. The sofa in our place folded out into a bed for him.

"I was thinking we could rent some movies, you know; take him to the zoo? The boy likes football." I rambled on while Glenn cracked his knuckles, still staring at the dark house. He talked about making a turkey, and I promised to help. I knew how to toss a salad. "We can get those foil pans with the sweet potatoes and marshmallows," I said.

"Did I tell you, Sam told me he loves me?" Glenn asked abruptly. "We were on the phone and then, *bam!*"—Glenn slammed his fist into his open palm and I jumped—"Just like that!" He turned to me, wonder in his face. "He's a good boy," he said. "I'd *pay* to spend time with that child." He swung the car door open, and the wind was as wet and real as raw meat.

It was 6 a.m. when we rang the bell. We'd made sure to block in the Camaro first—Glenn had warned me about "runners," though I hadn't seen one yet—and when Revere answered the door, a man with a chafed red face and tiny eyes, like a rhino, I think he took that in first: the big hulk of the Suburban, fencing in his ride. He was all in blue: navy sweat pants and a T-shirt and hoodie that strained across his belly, and he was at least a head taller than Glenn. Shaped almost like an almond, his head was, with those teeny eyes, comically small.

"We've come for the car, sir," Glenn said. He always started out polite, because you never knew.

"And who the hell are you?" In one ham fist, Revere gripped a coffee mug, leaking steam, and he took a sip from it, keeping his eyes on Glenn.

"Agent Grand, sir." Glenn loved this bit, the agent part— "Grand" was an alias and it let Glenn be whoever he wanted, a boy playing cops and robbers. Tilting his head, he looked Revere up and down. "I'm here about the car."

"The car," Revere repeated. He jerked his chin in my direction. "You in the habit of bringing little girls along to do a man's work?"

"I am no child, sir," I said, though truth be told I'd run into this before, because I'm a small person, and dress young. But I was twenty-two the day we met Revere. I had aspirations. "And I ain't no hack neither," I added, because he wouldn't look at me and didn't *that* piss me off.

Like his eyes, Revere's smile was piggy, revealing stumpy beige teeth. "Whatever." He took a closer look at Glenn and started to laugh. "What the hell, man! I *know* you. Grand, my ass!" They'd been in the joint together, Revere said, and if I hadn't been behind Glenn I wouldn't have seen how he took a step back. Revere opened the door to let us in: "Come on back, if you gotta." The door served right into the living room, which was neater than I might have guessed, nearly empty: a plush blue sofa and a plastic child's kitchen set, that's it. The rug was orange shag, matted and whorled; the American flag in the window cast its shade. The house smelled like a dog.

I waited for Glenn to say, *No sir; you must be mistaken. We'll wait right out here.* Rule number one: you never go inside. But Glenn cocked his head and stared at Revere for a moment, then laughed himself. "God*damn*," he whispered, stepping over the threshold. "It *is* you."

"So it's Grand now, huh?"

"Since when you been Revere?" Glenn answered back.

"Man's got to get a new start. Guess you and me both know that." And then Revere laughed again. I hovered behind them like a broken pull-toy, close enough to Glenn to touch his jacket—I hadn't known, of course, that he'd been to jail. "Come on back," Revere said, "but keep it down. I got a grandkid."

—

The kitchen gave the lie to that tidy living room: the counters were stacked with crusted dishes and pans half-full of food turned dark. Cigarette smoke stroked the air. Revere motioned us to a wood table with a scarred, blue-painted top and one missing leg; that table balanced in the middle of the room like some sort of weird bird. "Coffee?" he asked, and when we said sure, he fished two plastic mugs from the sink, rinsed them out and filled them from a pot on the stove. The coffee smelled good, but I left the cup where he set it; I could see dried ketchup, a little cloud of it dark as blood, where my mouth would have gone.

"Do you know this guy?" I hissed, though I guess I knew the answer. It made me mad, the way Glenn ignored me. He kept his eyes on Revere, lifting his cup to be hospitable, though I saw he didn't bring it near his lips.

"How you been, anyway?" Revere was making a show of rifling through drawers. There was a little kitchen desk made of pressed wood in one corner, the two drawers clogged with paper so that they didn't close, and Revere pulled at first one and then the other until there was the sound of ripping, and he worked one of them free. "Got my checkbook somewhere here; how much do I owe?"

Glenn pulled a folded paper from his breast pocket and smoothed it out on the table. "Says here you owe six grand, but it's too late for the money. *Sir*," he added politely. "Just the keys; you clear out any personals and we'll be off."

Revere whistled. "That much, huh?" He pinched a black plastic billfold out of the drawer clutter and held it up so we could see it. "Here we go. You sure about that amount?"

Glenn tapped the paper. "We can't take your money, Mr. Revere. That would be against the law."

"So it's Mr. Revere now, huh? No more Jack-o?" His face was sly, the skin stretched across it so tight it was almost shiny. Under that there was something else, depraved and mean. I've seen the prison shows, sure, and I wondered if Glenn and Revere had shared a cell. "We had us a time, huh? I lost touch with The Snapper. You keep in touch with The Snapper?"

"Been a long time," Glenn said. "The car, now—"

"Or Ryan? You hear from Ryan?"

"It's been a long time," Glenn repeated, deliberately.

"Guess you can tell me how you're doing, huh?" Revere slapped the three-legged table so that it tilted, dangerously. "You doing okay?"

Glenn made a show of looking around the room. "I guess I made something of myself," he said finally. "I work hard. I got me a son. Me and Astor, here, you should see our place. We got what, a buttload of cable channels, honey?" That did me in a little: Glenn never called me honey. I opened my mouth, weak with a rush of affection, but he didn't wait for my answer. "I done all right by myself," he said. "I made me a life." He was showing off, strutting like a bantam there in that shit kitchen in bumfuck Illinois.

"Your boss know you been in the joint?" Revere was smirking. I liked him for just that moment, asking what I wondered myself.

"Hey, there," Glenn said.

He was looking over my shoulder so I turned in my chair. A little boy, probably no older than five, stood in the doorway to the kitchen. He wore pajama bottoms printed with faded dinosaurs and a blue T-shirt that hung below his knees.

The child just gaped. Hugging himself, he moved into the kitchen and took a seat at the table between Glenn and me.

"Kid don't talk," Revere grunted. "Dumb as a post." I looked at the boy, who hung his head and stared at the tabletop, waiting. Revere put an opened box of cereal in front of him and a bowl from the sink. The child ignored the bowl and set right in, digging out handfuls of cereal from the box and shoving them into his mouth.

"Guess he's smart enough," Glenn said, nodding at the dirty bowl.

If the child heard what was going on, he didn't let on. He kept his eyes down, chewing fast, as if he guessed the cereal might go away again the way it had come.

"My daughter's boy. I get him when she works. And I mean *when*." Revere smirked, at no one in particular, then threw the plastic checkbook into the center of the table. It skidded past the little boy and stopped in front of Glenn, the plastic dented, patterned with diamonds. "This won't do ya anyway," Revere said, almost cheerfully. "I ain't got six grand in there."

A dog came skittering around the corner at us, a tiny thing with dirty white hair that stuck out around its face like the spokes of a wheel. I hate small dogs, and waited for Revere to drop kick it back to wherever it had come from, but he crouched down on his hams and petted the dog's ears, murmuring while it skipped and yapped.

"That's my baby, that's my baby," he said, and the dog quivered with delight. "Who's my little girl?" Revere repeated, again and again, and I exchanged looks with Glenn. "Are these people bothering you? Huh, sweetie? Huh?" Then the dog piddled, right there on the kitchen floor.

"You got debt," Glenn said to Revere, turning away from the dog's mess. "We got to take the car."

"I'm good for it," Revere said, standing and slapping his chest. That still haunts me, the way he did that. He was sure of himself, the way we all can be mistaken. "I didn't say I didn't have the money. I just don't got it *there*." He winked at the checkbook.

"I am not here to play games, Mr. Revere." The words were right, and usually this was the point when Glenn could get rough, but he was looking at the boy, mute in his chair. The kid's T-shirt hung off-kilter, his shoulder poking through the neck hole like something obscene.

"We don't usually come in-house," I added, to be helpful, but I might as well've been invisible, the notice those two took of me.

"I ain't playing games either. I guess you know me well enough to know that. I'm good for it, I tell you," the man said, asthma popping in his chest. Revere and Glenn looked each other over for a long moment. I should have dragged Glenn from the house. Balls to the wall. "Let's have some breakfast," Revere said. "I know a place we can talk. Catch up, like. Car ain't goin' nowhere."

"All right, then," Glenn finally said. "What the hell?" And he laughed, his face reckless and given over to something I didn't understand.

The two men stood and when Glenn finally gave me a look, I stood, too. When we left that kitchen, the child was still eating, piss on the floor. Glenn and I looked back at the boy, but Revere said, "We won't be but a minute. His grandma; she'd be around here somewhere."

—

I tried to pull Glenn aside between the house and the car—"What we doing, honey? Who is this guy?"—but he just told me, *hush.*

Maybe he didn't say it quite so friendly. We piled into Glenn's Suburban, which Glenn always said gave him what he called a seriousness: "Me being a family man and all." I went to the second row of seats, behind Revere, just trying to keep out of the way. We were silent all the way to the restaurant, and then, as it turned out, the place was closed: it wasn't but 7 o'clock.

Glenn turned away, drumming his fingers on the wheel. "Well I'm sorry," he said, not sounding it. "We've got other clients to see. We'll go back now, take the car."

"There's another place! What're you saying? We go back, you and me. Don't that count for anything?" Revere pulled the soft collar of his sweatshirt away from his neck and shook his head, once and then twice. His cheek was the color of a brick.

Glenn was off his game today, I could see. And Revere. That one: I didn't want *him* coming unglued. He was one of the freaky ones, I could already tell; there was the jail business, and Glenn had told me about clients carrying guns. In my own family I was always the one could smooth things over, so I leaned forward between the two men, who sat in a troubling quiet, and said the first thing that came to me: that we could get some steak, some coffee, before any more business had to be done. "You like coffee, right?" I asked. "I'm good for shit if I don't have at least two cups; just can't think worth a damn. Fuck, I can't do anything! How 'bout you?"

I was babbling, talking foul to make them listen, and for the first time Revere really looked at me, grinning through his hatred. He had gold in his teeth, I saw, gleaming dull from the wet hole of his mouth.

"This other place, it'll be open," he said.

Glenn stared straight ahead, but he started the car. I take

responsibility for that, for getting him to breakfast. At the time I just thought how the day was shot to hell.

—

The morning smelled like snow when we pulled into the lot of a restaurant called MaryPat's. Cutouts of pilgrims and happy turkeys, greened from the sun, were taped onto the plate glass. They made me sad, somehow.

We piled out of the car, and I peered through the window at the brown plastic booths. "Look there," I said to Glenn. "We can get ourselves a corner booth." He made as if to nod at me, his face empty and distracted, then elbowed past to lead the way inside. A bored waitress greeted us. Her pink smock was stained, her jowls whiskered and quivering, but she led us to the corner booth and I took that to be a good omen.

Outside the sun was trying. I told the waitress we'd all have coffee and she poured, her face sour. Studying his menu, Glenn was mute, but he looked up when Revere started whistling, just under his breath: something tuneless. *Ugly*, I thought, but Glenn had the barest smile.

"You still singing that damn song?" he asked, and he laid the menu aside.

"Hell, yeah!" Revere said.

After we ordered steak and eggs, hash and potato, Glenn's cell rang, and he excused himself: "It's Carly," he said to me. I watched him walk away; standing in the corner by the gum machine, he bowed his head to hear and waved his free arm. I tried to think what a man like Glenn would go to prison for: what did they call it when it wasn't so bad, really? Glenn must've done something bad with paper or numbers, something to do with what I'd heard him call "loopholes."

Revere started talking again. Pressing the tabletop with his fingers, he told me he had a glass eye. "Tell which is the fake one," he said to me. "Tell which." Revere's face was pitted around his mouth. It was a little mouth, sunken and puckered. "Mouth like a cunt": that was an expression I'd heard Glenn use, talking about a folk singer we both hated, although at the time I hadn't understood what he meant. Looking at Revere, I knew.

"Your left," I said, though I knew it was the right. I could see how dead the right eye was, filmed over like a pond in August.

"Ha!" Revere cried out in triumph. The waitress laid our plates before us.

Glenn came back to the table, his face hard. He pushed into the booth and stabbed at his egg.

"So," Revere said. "We got ourselves a little reunion here."

"Guess *you* been a busy boy," Glenn said. His voice was flat. "Grandkids."

"I got me a life," Revere agreed. "Once the bank's open I can get you your cash."

"How old is your grandson, sir?"

Revere thought for a moment, and when he answered his voice was careless and stumped. "I'd say five, give or take." Revere scraped at the juice on his plate with a spoon. "Kid don't talk," he said, shrugging.

"You said that before," Glenn said. "What's he like? What's his name?"

"His mother named him something foolish. I call him Roy." Bored, Revere turned his attention to the meat on his plate, sawing at it with a dinner knife that shone soft in his hand. I looked at my own knife and it was the same, its cutting blade luminous and the handle, made of weightier stuff than you might expect, swirled white, like the inside of an oyster.

"Children are precious," Glenn said. "They don't ask to be here." He stirred at his food with the wrong end of a spoon, then looked up sharply. "Do you love your grandson, sir?"

"Jesus loves the little children," Revere sang, spearing his meat and lifting it to his mouth.

"I love my son," Glenn said. "I love him more than my life."

Revere shrugged again. "I got two grand." He looked past us, out the window, at the broken street.

"Look!" I said, and held up my knife, rubbing my thumb along that pearled handle. "Pretty fine for a place like this, huh?" As if I could distract them. That kind of money would buy Glenn time with his son. And what would happen if he took the money? I didn't know, and I was afraid.

Glenn licked his lips and smiled tightly at me before turning his attention back to Revere, who chewed and stared back at him, insolence in his face. Wind sprayed grit against the window, rattling its frame. "You are no kind of man," Glenn said. He pushed his plate away, the coils of hash so stiff with grease they looked shellacked. He folded his arms over his chest.

"You're one to talk." Revere's voice, lazy, troubling, was obscured by a mouthful of meat. He chewed slowly, then swallowed. "Aren't you the big man? A *repo* man?" He turned to me, his dead eye winking. "Man tells me I'm nothing! Can you imagine that? Guess my money might be good enough for him though, huh? Eh?" Revere grunted, and the meat on his plate swam in its juices.

"I'm not ashamed of what I do," Glenn said.

"Guess you'll say next that you're what—*proud?*" Revere snorted. "Proud of taking out from under decent folks when they hit a rough patch?" He looked around the empty diner, mock-horror on his face. "Will you get a load of this, ladies and gentlemen? Excuse me, but this here is a *real* man!" Of the handful of people in the place, only one looked up: a middle-aged woman in a man's buffalo plaid, her drooping eye making her seem sad, and wiser than she probably was.

The waitress came by with the check and gave us a look.

"I believe the lady wants her table freed up," Revere said, winking at her broad pink back. "Fraid I don't have any cash on me; guess I'll go wait by the car."

He stood and pushed a toothpick between his lips, patches of red simmering in his elephant cheeks, then swaggered out of the restaurant.

"God damn! God damn this ugly world!" Glenn stood, and I had to look away from the grief in his face.

"You don't have to do this," I said. "Honey, you don't need that money!"

"Stay the fuck out of my affairs, missy," he said, and his voice was mean the way I'd heard it once or maybe twice before. Then I might have deserved it, but this time was different: I wasn't bitching about Carly, or the smell of Marlboros in the drapes. "How do you know what I need?"

"You two need help?" the waitress called. Her voice was high. "I could get my manager, you two need help."

"We're fine," I said. I took Glenn's arm and held to it.

"That bitch," Glenn said, and though he might have meant the waitress I knew he meant Carly. He swept his coat from the seat, rolling it in his arms. "I've got you, though," he said to me.

"You're my world, aren't you? Aren't you?" He squeezed my shoulders, joylessly.

"I am," I said, walking him to the door. I knew myself to be important just then. In that moment, before it all went to hell, I felt good, like I could handle whatever came next.

Outside the wind had picked up, throwing trash around the empty lot. Revere was waiting by the Suburban, hands in his pockets, hoodie zipped to his thick neck. "I thank you for my breakfast, kind sir," he said.

There wasn't anything to say to that, so we got in the car. "It cannot be denied that I am a good father," Glenn said. He sat at the wheel, staring straight ahead. "I have made an effort all of my life. I tried to build something. I'm a decent man."

"Sure you are, captain," Revere said. "Bank's this way." From the passenger seat he gestured broadly to the right, where a bank, next to a hardware store, made up most of the downtown. But Glenn drove through the blinking yellow intersection, past a few more clumps of storefront and two straggling blocks of frame houses listing on their foundations like boats. Nothing had legs in this town; the fields of corn, all those furrowed rows hardened by frost, came soon after.

"Town's that way," Revere said, twisting in his seat. "Ain't gonna get my money, driving out here."

Glenn didn't say anything and I was powerful relieved: so we were going back for the car, after all.

"A man would already have paid his way," Glenn said through his teeth, which were yellow-white. I'd seen them up close; I had licked them with desire. Outside the window were the rows of corn, stripes of caramel and then iced land, like a cake. Glenn jerked the wheel hard to the right and the car skittered along the gravel shoulder. He just meant to scare Revere, to best him. I still believe that.

"What, tough guy?" Revere thrust his chin out at Glenn. "We gonna have at it, what, out in the cornfield?" When he laughed he wheezed.

Glenn stepped from the car like he hadn't a care. Revere followed, rolling his shoulders, and when they faced each other it could have been comical, a silly Western, except for the way Glenn's mouth drew down and into itself. I opened the door, but something made me stay where I was, one leg in, one leg out, a hand shading my eyes because the sun was clearing the sky with a white light but no heat. I think it was all that land, the weight of it, that stopped me. There was nothing out there to hold back the wind, not a building, not a tree, and I felt as though I couldn't breathe.

Neither of them was built to fight. Glenn was small but soft, not wiry, and Revere was too big, run to fat. They circled each other like dogs, necks stiff, not relaxed or easy, though once in a while someone's fist would make contact and the sound was a wonder: dull, and louder than you might think. They were sweating, but since no one was getting seriously hurt, I could still say, "Stop, you guys, just *stop*," without feeling I had to do more. I even remember thinking, *hell, let them get it out of their systems, before we have to take the car.*

When Revere got a lucky punch in, sending Glenn staggering, he leaned forward, hands on his knees, his laughter bubbling through that pocked, defective chest. "Guess you and me is just alike, even after all these years, huh?" He kept laughing, shaking his head. "A *repo* man. Jesus!"

Glenn regained his footing, and when he cried out, his voice was angry, almost scared-sounding: "I am nothing like you! *Nothing!*" There was mud on his shoes, a streak of it on his cheek, and when he brought out the dinner knife, pearled and terrible from wherever he had stashed it, he might have been crying.

"Hey, big man, you don't think you're going to use that, do you?" Revere said. He swiped at the knife, almost knocking it from Glenn's fist. The handle caught the light. "Yeah," Revere said, waggling his hips like a woman. "You don't got the balls."

"Shut up!" I said to Revere, and stepped toward them, mincing like a scared horse, red fireworks behind my eyes because then I knew.

Glenn jabbed at Revere frantically, and when the knife caught the big man in the arm, blood bloomed. "I. Am. Nothing. Like. You!" he screamed.

"Hey!" Revere called, and for the first time he sounded uncertain. "Enough. Okay? So I'm a fat fuck; what do you care what I think?" He broke away, then ran toward the Suburban, but his bulk slowed him and Glenn was at his heels like a terrier, face contorted. "Remember how The Boss, he used to beg us to run so he could shoot us?" Revere's voice was pleading through the horrible wet froth of his asthma, and the dinner knife, it moved so quickly I couldn't see it. Revere couldn't either; it was his blind side, though he made it as far as the front passenger door, dragging it open. He didn't have a chance. Clumsy with terror, he scrabbled at the step, and through the gray brush of his hair I could see a glint of scalp before the knife, slashing, made a ripe, bright sound and Revere grunted, once. He dropped like a stone. My God, the blood. Freshets of it, gouting bright as paint over the Suburban, over the iced ground, and over the pajama-print palms on Glenn's shirt that I'd pressed that morning.

Revere rocked on the ground where he'd fallen, and Glenn dropped the knife. "You okay?" he asked Revere, and the man burbled, like water over stones. I turned my face away, ashamed for him, for the noise he made. Revere took his breath in then, and was still.

"Oh man, I'm sorry," Glenn said.

Revere's body lay half out of the car, and Glenn pushed it all the way out before slamming the door. The body rolled down the gravel embankment, crushing tall brown grass that crackled even as it hid him.

I never screamed, and I still don't know why. Glenn's face was perfectly still. "I won't tell," I said, watching him try to kick grass over the blood on the ground, even as I marked the place in my mind. They found the knife there later, when they found Revere.

Glenn is in the state prison over in Joliet, I made sure of that. He was right about me, after all. Balls to the wall. Even the cops treated me with respect. I was important to them, until I wasn't.

We drove for an hour without speaking, passing through woods that another time would have seemed beautiful to Glenn and so to me: I was starting to recognize the things that moved him. Light running over branches, and the hard shapes of the trees. In my lap, my hands jerked. When we were through the woods Glenn pulled the car over, abruptly, and slammed the wheel with his palms.

"Was prison like the movies?" I asked. All that had happened, and still I had to know. I thought things might still, somehow, be right between us.

"The man was scum," was all he said, then he put his head in his hands and I saw how it was. He'd tried to be the man, hadn't he, grit in his belly, in the red-rubber chambers of his heart?

When he pulled his hands away I saw that they were black with blood.

I miss him, I do. I would say I love him. You ask how that can be so, but things could just as easily have gone the other way: Glenn on the ground, face to the sky while life lapped out of him. The man had goodness in him, as well as that cruel despair, and the two come from the same place, don't you think?

"I am the repo man," he said, but he was lost to me then. Behind us were the trees, tough little maples that shivered and clacked; I twisted in my seat to watch them until we were done waiting there, and Glenn started the car, so the next part could begin.

Dinosaurs

The signs began to appear ten miles before we got to the entrance, hand-painted billboards of smiling dinosaurs in outrageous colors: *Only eight more miles until you hit Terra Dinosaur. Raaaar! Six more miles and you'll be battling the mighty T. rex!* Even so, we missed the turnoff, which we realized when we saw another sign: *You have just passed Terra Dinosaur! Turn back, oh man!* It wasn't Floyd's fault: the turnoff was a driveway, long and graveled and lined with disreputable-looking palm trees. The entrance sign had blown over and was partially obscured by vegetation. My mother-in-law, Dolores, tilted back her hat, its floppy, green-straw brim faded almost to yellow, ribbons tied under her chin.

"Goodness, Floyd!" she said. "We must put our best foot forward!"

This was a favorite expression of hers. She'd said exactly the same thing to me every morning of our visit so far, when she appeared at breakfast in full makeup: peachy foundation and a dense tangerine lipstick that glistened like oil. I had become lazy, pulling my hair back into a ponytail and leaving my eyes and lips bare. When I look back at pictures from that time, I see that my hair and skin were as dull as clay. I didn't know then how grief had aged me.

—

"Tidy as a bean," Dolores said approvingly of the modest, white-stuccoed house at the end of the driveway. More tired palms were out front, along with another dinosaur cutout, this one fixed in the ground with a wooden stake: *Welcome to Terra Dinosaur! We offer summer rates!* The gravel parking area to the right of the house was empty. Floyd pulled in and turned off the car, sighing. The air conditioning shut off with a hiss.

"Where are we?" Gil asked, rubbing his eyes. It was the summer before his sixth birthday. He'd fallen asleep in the booster seat I'd hauled down from Minneapolis, his cheek striped red from the seat belt. I helped him unbuckle and tried to ignore the headache starting its slow, dull march across the back of my skull.

"We're here!" Dolores trilled. "Wake up, little man!"

"Where are the dinosaurs?" Gil looked at the house, which gleamed like a tooth under the Florida sun.

Floyd grunted something unintelligible.

"Oh, you," Dolores said to her husband. "Look, here comes someone now!"

A man about Floyd's age was picking his way across the parking area in bare feet. Narrow in build, and balding, he wore dress pants hoisted nearly to chest level and a tank top bleached as white as the house.

"Hello, folks!" He shaded his eyes, peering at us. "Have you come to see the dinosaurs?" He pronounced it "dinno-sours."

No, I wanted to say, *we've come to talk politics.* I opened the car door and swung my legs into the sun. "My boy would like to see some dinosaurs," I said.

"You've come to the right place, then," the man assured me. He reached into his pants pocket and withdrew a round tin; still smiling, he tucked a chaw of tobacco into his cheek. "Five dollars a head," he said, chomping peaceably.

"You can't beat *that* price," my mother-in-law said.

We all got out of the Crown Victoria and stood in the sopping heat while the man explained that there were no guided tours of the park; we were free to walk through it at our own pace. "We've got snacks in the house. You come by and see us after. Name's Marsden," he said, patting his spindly chest. "My wife is Therese." He pocketed the twenty Floyd had given him and nodded toward a crushed-shell path that wound behind the house. "Just follow that there; you'll see what to do."

Marsden hobbled back over the stones to the lawn; when he reached the grass, he turned back and saluted us. "Stay on the path, that's all I ask. You have a good time now, hear? Raaaarrrrr!"

Floyd shook his head and took Gil's hand. "Well, at least we know who painted the signs," he said under his breath. "C'mon, son, let's get a move on."

—

My husband, Brian—the Hockings' only child—had been dead six months that summer Gil and I traveled to Florida.

"Come," Floyd had said gently the night he'd called to invite us, his grief a vivid thrumming across the phone line. Brian had died unexpectedly at age thirty, a week before my twenty-eighth birthday, from a brain aneurysm that burst like a blister while he was shoveling snow off the roof of the old Victorian we were fixing up. We'd been married six years and were living in Minneapolis, the city we had adopted after Brian got a high school teaching job there. The two of us staked out favorite bookstores—the ones with couches and cats—and coffeehouses where they made the coffee so strong I would fill half the cup with cream to dilute it. Then Gil was born.

We hadn't had much contact with Brian's parents during that time; he said he loved them, and I believe he did, but his mother was "demanding," as Brian put it. He shrugged when he said it; we were just starting a life that didn't have anything to do with them. Perhaps it would have been different if they'd lived closer. But they were in Florida, where Brian had grown up, a place almost exotic to me, with its palms and surf and white sand. They sent a Christmas letter every year with a crate of oranges and a standing invitation to visit, but we'd never gotten around to it, and then Brian died.

When Floyd called, I didn't recognize at first the clear, low baritone of his voice. "We'd like to spend some time with you and the boy," he said. "Get to know you better."

I felt guilty, because it was true: we hardly knew one another. Since Brian's death I had found a modicum of comfort in my girlfriends, none of whom had children, some of whom were divorced and needed me as much as I suddenly needed them. But they pitched in willingly enough: a tribe of women helping to raise my five-year-old boy. My own mother and father were dead, and, like Brian, I was an only child, born late to aging parents. Gripping the phone that night with Brian's father on the other end—Gil was in bed, and I had carefully allotted myself first one, then two glasses of cheap wine while the television quaked with canned laughter—I felt regret that I hadn't reached out myself. When Floyd offered to fly Gil and me down to Florida for two weeks, I calculated my vacation time from my job at the library and decided that both of us could use a change of scenery.

At Brian's funeral Gil had let Dolores hold his hand; she'd wiped the snot from his nose and drawn the hair out of his eyes with a wet comb. On the flight down I remembered the clean lines in my son's hair and felt grateful.

When we arrived in Florida, my in-laws found us at the baggage claim, and it seemed at first that the visit could be a success. They were touchingly nervous, and they'd dressed carefully: Floyd in pressed khakis and Dolores in a coral dress. Her dyed hair escaped from under her scarf, and when she leaned close, I could see that the fabric was patterned with parrots. *She likes birds*, I thought. Something to talk about later.

"Dolores!" I said, and she gave me a kiss that left orange crescents on my cheek.

They'd brought Gil a balloon and a book about dinosaurs, lavishly illustrated, which we ended up reading in the food court at the airport. Floyd treated—pizza slices all around—and as I watched my quiet son grow expansive, even loquacious, under their attention, I felt sure I'd made the right decision to come.

It wasn't until we got to their place that my good mood started to flag: the house was small, smelling of camphor, its rooms stuffed with furniture and bric-a-brac owls. I was used to small homes—before Brian and I bought the decrepit Victorian, I had lived in a series of closet-sized apartments—but here it felt different: a cramping of the spirit, maybe. I tried to imagine Brian here—as a boy and as a college student, returning home—but I couldn't.

"So, you like birds," I said that first night, pretending to study a ceramic owl that hung over the kitchen door.

"Not really," Dolores said. She'd taken off her shoes and was padding around the kitchen in nyloned feet. "Skit-scat-scoot!" she chirped, and I stepped aside so that she could pull a series of casserole dishes from a cabinet. Balancing the bowls, she straightened and followed my gaze to the owl. "Oh, that," she said. "It's just something to hang up. I always try to have a theme." I thought about my kitchen at home, the Buddha tacked over the drainboard, the photos on the fridge. "Everyone needs a theme," she continued in an instructive tone. "I decided a long time ago that owls would be mine."

———

The dinosaurs were made of cement, as lumpy and gray as porridge, with a chicken-wire infrastructure that poked through in places. The park was bigger than it had first appeared, with dinosaurs around every turn: sparring triceratopses, their horns metal tubes painted an improbable gold; a squat, unidentified dinosaur armored with hubcaps, on whose concrete flanks someone had scrawled, *Lenny Sux.* Marsden had taken care with the landscaping, the palm trees set at regular intervals. There was a sagging chain-link fence, the wire bubbled with rust, and beyond it, what looked like swamp extending to infinity.

"Mama, these dinosaurs are weird," Gil whispered. Floyd had

moved ahead to study a brachiosaurus, its sagging midsection propped up by a two-by-four. Dolores lagged behind, adjusting her hat.

"Do you like them?" I whispered back.

"I don't know," he said, his face worried.

I tried not to dwell on the fact that I was using up my vacation time in this place, reminding myself we couldn't afford to go anywhere else anyway. My headache flowered darkly at the back of my neck. I fumbled in my purse, hoping to find a few aspirin.

Dolores caught up with us then. "Isn't this charming?" she said. "Just good, simple fun!"

"Uh-huh," Gil agreed dutifully. He'd brought his plastic triceratops from the car and was clutching it to his chest. I noticed then how shaggy his hair had gotten. Brian used to cut Gil's hair, lifting our son to a stool in the basement and pinning a sheet around his neck before setting to work, and I realized with panicky resignation that I hadn't taken Gil to the barber since. In the Florida humidity his fine hair thickened and frizzed like foam around his face, and though I started to put out my hand to stroke the strands away from his cheeks, I was overcome with such lethargy due to the burning, wet day that I let my arm fall back down.

———

Dinner at the Hockings' that first night had been pot roast and gravy; we ate in the dining room, which was so cluttered with furniture that we had to slip into our chairs sideways. The tabletop was hardly visible, loaded as it was with meat and potatoes; a cold salad bristling with tiny, hard marshmallows; and bowl after bowl of vegetables, luminous with butter. It was all served up on the good china.

"I think it's nicer, don't you?" Dolores said, and I was charmed at first, not realizing that the gold pattern on the dishes meant they'd all have to be hand-washed. "That's *our* job," she sang out to me after we ate. "You boys go watch TV!" Gil, who never escaped chores at home and who always carefully negotiated his television privileges, leapt up, flashing me an incredulous look that said he couldn't believe his luck.

In the kitchen I scraped and stacked the dishes, the smile on my face fixed. I leaned past Dolores at the sink to rinse the gluey gravy from the plates.

"Gil has the soul of his father," Dolores said, shifting to one hip to give me access. "He's a Hocking, all right."

"I see his father in him," I agreed carefully.

"You take Brian at this age: I could not *tear* that child away from the television!" Dolores nodded at the darkened living room. I could just make out Floyd and Gil sitting next to each other on the couch, rapt, their faces washed with the TV's cold, blue light.

"Gil doesn't actually watch much television," I murmured, but Dolores cut me off with a laugh.

"Just like his father!" she said, as if she hadn't heard me. She stared out the window. I saw the dime-sized age spots on her neck. I saw the sadness in her. "They get away from you," Dolores said.

But then she turned to me, and her face had restored itself; her eyes sparkled bright and hard. "Now, it's none of my business, but you have a boy like that, and you need to take care."

"Take care?"

"Take care," Dolores said firmly. "Or you'll lose him." She took up the stack of clean dishes and put them away.

"He isn't lost," I said. "He's with me." Despite my best efforts, my voice wavered.

"Boys, men, they're all alike," Dolores said, lowering her voice to a conspiratorial whisper. "You never have them, you know." She straightened up and nodded curtly at me. "They aren't yours."

"I never supposed . . ." The plates in my hands clacked together like castanets, and with brisk efficiency she whisked them to safety. "He's five," I whispered.

"Who wants dessert?" she called into the living room, already piling raisin cookies onto a plate.

"I'll take them," I said, intending to squeeze between Gil and Floyd on the sofa and stay there until bedtime, sucking those cookies down one by one. But I had only just stepped into the living room with the plate when Dolores caught my arm with a surprisingly strong grip. Her nails were long; she probably didn't mean for them to cut into the soft underside of my arm.

She took the plate from my hands and deposited it in Gil's lap. "Eat!" she said, and then to me, "Let's leave the boys to their fun."

Back in the kitchen, at a table of gray-specked Formica, she opened a photo album covered in gilt. Outside, the low sun was loose and mellow. This was the hard time, the end of the day. Brian and I used to watch movies after Gil was in bed. We ate ice cream out of soup bowls. We shared a blanket on the couch and made fun of ourselves: how much we loved bad movies, how much we loved each other.

"Here's my boy!" Dolores said, and I dragged my attention back to the album. "See, there's Gil, right there in my Brian's face!" She tapped the page. It was true. I might have been holding a picture of Gil in my hands: the same narrow, almost patrician nose; the same fine brown hair, brightened to red in places. The young Brian sat before a plate heaped with pancakes. Behind him a pretty, youngish woman with bright lips hovered, hands twisted in her apron. The happiness of the boy in the photo surprised me. "His birthday," murmured Dolores. "I always made him pancakes for his birthday as a special treat."

I'd forgotten that Brian once had freckles like Gil.

Dolores was watching me, arms folded across her chest. "For the first years of his life, it was the 'Brian and Dolores Show,'" she said. "That's what we used to say! Floyd worked a lot. It was the boy and me. I knew what made him happy." She brushed at her breast where crumbs from the raisin cookies clung. "Pancakes," she said. "He loved pancakes on his birthday. Did you know that? Did you two make pancakes, in your little love nest?"

I was shocked at the hate in her voice.

—

Terra Dinosaur was Dolores' idea; she'd dismissed the Disney World brochures I'd packed, with a smirking reference to how expensive it was. My face burned; a part of me had hoped Floyd would offer to pay. At Disney World my son would have been riding a roller coaster by now. He would have been shaking Mickey's hand.

"I'm hungry, Mama," Gil said. Sulking, he shook loose from me. We were standing next to a stegosaurus, an odd creature, stupidly ugly: four stumpy legs and the head like a fifth, welded to the ground as if it were eating bracken. Cracks in the cement plates along its back looked like the dark veins of a leaf. Gil picked up a stick and whacked the stegosaurus, hard. "I'm hungry!" he screamed.

Giving in to my headache, I turned to him and said, "Jesus, Gil! Enough already! Go ask your grandpa to get you something." I couldn't see Floyd on the path anymore, but he had to be just up ahead. "Here." I grabbed Gil's arm, harder than I meant to, and pressed a few dollars into his hand. "Get yourselves something cool to drink. It's hot as hell out here."

Dolores caught up to me, and we watched Gil run up the path, legs pumping; it was obvious he was grateful to escape. "What did I tell you?" she said. She pretended to study the stegosaurus.

"Excuse me?"

She shrugged, running her hand along the dinosaur's side, as if to comfort the beast. "I'm just saying: What goes around comes around."

"Gil is a good kid," I said tightly.

"Oh, well, so was Brian, my dear. But then they grow up and away, don't they?" She squinted down the path at the scrim of dust Gil had kicked up, then back at me. My son was nowhere in sight. "Some of them sooner than others, I dare say." She opened her handbag and, without taking her eyes from my face, extracted a mint and popped it into her mouth.

"We're fine!" I shot back before turning and striding ahead, the crushed shell of the path working its way into my flip-flops. I wouldn't stop to shake them clean; I wasn't going to give her that satisfaction.

"I always thought my Brian would marry . . . oh, someone different!" she called after me.

I stopped and turned. "He did all right for himself," I said.

And then, because I was mean from grief, I yelled what I thought might hurt her most: "You want to know something? Gil and I are closer than you and Brian ever were. Okay? And at least I used to call my mother. I visited my parents until the day they died."

I didn't wait for an answer but surged up the path, certain that I had reclaimed something lost to me. My head pounded so hard I thought I might vomit. I needed aspirin and thought maybe they had some at the house. I thought about changing our flight reservations, heading home early. I thought a lot of things.

—

"Are you having fun?" I had asked Gil on the fourth day of our visit. We had spent a lot of time at the house, preparing elaborate meals. That day we had finally gone out, to the mall and a McDonald's, but now the TV already hummed in the next room, and the evening stretched ahead of us, so heavy with boredom I had to work to ignore a rising tide of panic. We were in the guest room, and Gil was playing with the Matchbox cars he'd brought, pushing them along the worn corduroy ribs of the bedspread. "Are you looking forward to the dinosaur park?" I said. "Grandpa says it's not a long drive. Maybe an hour. We can go tomorrow, he says. Or the next day."

"I like Grandpa better than Grandma," Gil said, not taking his eyes off the shiny purple car.

"Why do you say that?" I asked, my voice too loud. I was already proven guilty, I thought: Gil must have caught on to my feelings about Brian's mother.

"He misses Daddy," Gil said, running the car into a boxy ambulance. "Boom!" he said.

"Have you talked to Grandma and Grandpa about your dad?"
I shifted so that I sat cross-legged like Gil.

"A little. Grandpa's sad about Dad," Gil said, pausing to look up at me. "He said, 'Listen to your mom.'"

By God, I loved that man. "And Grandma?" My voice skittered high. "What does Grandma say?"

I watched Gil back the cars up, repositioning them for another run-in. "Boom!" he said, not looking at me.

"What did Grandma say?" I looked around the tiny room, at our suitcases spilling cheap summer clothes onto the beds, then stood abruptly and picked at a shirt of Gil's. Wrinkled but clean, it was patterned with bulldozers. Lord, he was just a child. I folded the shirt hastily, pressing it back with the others. "You miss Daddy, I know," I said. "Did you want to talk about that?"

"Boom," my son whispered, lowering his head.

—

Marsden and Therese's front office was comfortable enough, with a couch, a few chairs, and a glass counter that ran the length of the room, filled with faded candy boxes. A vending machine stood in the corner. Floyd was sitting with his feet up, a Pepsi in one hand and a licorice wand in the other, talking to Marsden, who leaned against the counter, chewing meditatively. A coarse-featured woman stood in the doorway. She was younger than Marsden by some years, with a calm expression on her plain face and dark hair pulled back into a knot.

"Hi," she said. "I'm Therese." She wiped her hands on her jeans and held one out to me. "You must be Elizabeth. We've been enjoying your father-in-law here."

"Gil with his grandma?" Floyd asked. He looked relaxed, almost happy. *Being away from Dolores could do that to a person*, I thought bitterly.

"No. I thought he was with you," I said. For a moment we looked at each other. "Gil?" I asked the room. My voice was barely discernible over the pounding of my head, the sudden pounding of my heart.

"Now, a boy will wander," Marsden said reasonably.

We went outside, and there was Dolores, walking up the path with her hands on her hips.

"The boy's missing," Floyd told her.

She stood so still, Dolores did. She stared at me until I had to look away.

"We'll find him," Marsden said.

We walked the pathways, calling Gil's name as we retraced our steps: back past the stegosaurus with the cracked plates, circling a T. rex I hadn't noticed before. The tyrannosaurus might have been Marsden's masterpiece. It towered over me, a good ten feet tall, its eye a blue reflector that winked in the light, its considerable mouth gaping, revealing rows of tin-plate teeth as sharp as razor wire.

"How safe *is* this place?" I asked Marsden.

He and Therese exchanged glances. "I wouldn't worry, except for the gators," Marsden mumbled. He lit up a cigarette, glancing over the wire fence. I followed his eyes across the swampy scrub.

"Hush, the boy is fine," Therese soothed.

"Gil!" I shrieked. We circled the grounds twice, then checked the house: the refreshment area and the living room beyond. My son was sturdy, tall for his age, but he was not immune to disaster; no one was. Hadn't recent events taught me that?

Therese made us sit down in the front office after we'd searched for almost half an hour and Floyd's face had flushed a dangerous red, but I wouldn't take the chair she offered. My mother-in-law collapsed into the seat instead, her skirt riding up so that I could see her varicose veins. Therese pressed sodas into our hands, then held a handkerchief under the water tap and laid it across Floyd's forehead. "Let's think this through," she said.

I looked at Dolores, then away. She had been oddly silent, her mouth drawn down to a dot. I thought about saying something to her, but I was consumed by the moment: my only child, gone. There was no room for anything else.

—

Gil had been hiding in Marsden's workshop, a shed set back in a patch of weeds where he built the dinosaurs, and the one place we hadn't checked. Marsden routinely locked the door, but my son had climbed in through a window propped open with a concrete block. He had crouched in the cool, dusty darkness, behind a frame of rusted chicken wire, until he got bored and decided to find out if we'd missed him.

"You yelled at me when I said I was hungry," he accused me after he came to us, pushing through the front door of the house without apology. His hair was white with plaster dust.

I hugged my son, and there was the joy of his body yielding against mine. Behind me Marsden and Therese made cooing sounds that might have been expressions of their own relief: no missing children, no senior citizens with heatstroke, no lawsuits.

"I want to go home!" Gil said. "This place is dumb!"

"Gil," I said, because I felt I must, but then Dolores spoke.

"I don't understand," she said, her voice low. "Brian loved this place." Though I had not caught her crying, her makeup was blotchy, mascara smudged under her eyes.

"Are you all right?" I made myself ask her. She still clutched her untouched soda.

"I envy you," she said, her voice jittery.

I reached for her arm, but she turned to her husband.

"She was with him at the end," she said to Floyd. "Our son."

"It's all right," he said, and, putting his arm around her, he drew her close. His face had resumed something of its characteristic pallor, and in it I saw a sorrowful tenderness. I saw that he loved her.

"I lost my only child." Dolores' hands flapped a little. "He wasn't done yet, you know." Her voice was dry. "In the end we're alone, aren't we?" She nodded into her husband's shoulder.

"We came here when Brian was a little younger than Gil," Floyd said to us. "We came here, once."

Suddenly Dolores straightened and shook off Floyd's arm. "It was a long time ago," she said briskly. Then she turned to my son. "You shouldn't scare your mother like that. With all she does for you! What would your father think?" Her voice carried the same grating remonstrance it had all these long days of our visit, but for some reason it no longer bothered me.

"Papa isn't here!" Gil burst out.

"We all miss him," I said quickly, speaking into my son's hair. It smelled like celery. I caught Dolores' wet, frantic eyes with my own and held them.

"When does that stop?" Gil asked. He didn't cry, but he gripped my hand.

"I don't know," I admitted, before Dolores had to.

What I didn't tell him was that you never get over some things. You might learn to live with them, because you have to, but that's not the same. I think Dolores and I both understood that.

"Enough," she said, her cheeks as red and stippled as if they'd been slapped. I tried to imagine Dolores as a young woman, though I could not. Ardent, I supposed. Hopeful, before life's losses had begun to add up.

"I wish I'd known that your son loved pancakes," I offered. I stopped short of calling her "Mother" or "Mom"; she wasn't *my* mother, although probably nothing would have meant so much to her as calling her by the name that restored her to her best self. What generosity I did extend was born of pity, I suppose, a winner's sense of luck.

Because for right now, at least, I still had my Gil.

—

We bought ice cream from Marsden and Therese, and Gil and the Hockings and I took our cones, stuck with wet paper from the wrappers, onto the sweltering front porch. We held them out over the rail, the drips catching in the grass below. Just beyond was a canal filled with water as dark as tar. Birds with straw legs shrieked and walked through that dark water.

We would never be this close again, the four of us; I think I knew that even then. We stood in a row, as if the days, the years left to each of us would not take us in separate directions—and the strange birds of that place called to us as we were, shoulders almost touching, united in our magnificent isolation.

Acknowledgements

This book has taken shape over many years. I am indebted to countless individuals, only a few of whom I have space to acknowledge here. All of the stories got their start in Fred Shafer's short story workshop, and have been informed by Fred's incisive, thoughtful take on story writing, and by the work of the many excellent authors he brought in for us to meet. I am grateful for the experiences I had in his class, and for my continuing friendship with Fred, who remains my writing mentor today. I made many friends in this workshop, who have encouraged and supported me and my writing over the years: Vivian DeGraff; Fran Dvorak; Valerie Ellis; Jan English Leary; Mary Jo Kanady, who has welcomed me into her warm kitchen for writing dates with good biscotti and even better coffee; Marika Lindholm, whose writer gatherings were fun and also crucial to the development of many of these stories; Marylee MacDonald; Jill Pollack, StoryStudio Chicago founder and director, whose belief in and enthusiasm for my work encouraged me to do my first reading; Katherine Shonk, who has patiently read and re-read these stories more times than I can count; Lee Strickland; and Sue Tague, who came up with the story name from which the title of this book was drawn. Some of these individuals have also been part of CafeGrrls, a community of writers that provided valuable feedback on my work and expanded my writing network to include friends and writers Julie Justicz, Jackie Keer, and Lynn Sloan. My sincere thanks to you all.

In my days as a librarian at DePaul University in Chicago, I had the good fortune to work with dedicated professionals who inspired me with their curiosity about the world, and aided me in research that leant veracity to my stories. My direct bosses and friends Paula Dempsey and Arlie Sims didn't bat an eye when I asked to take a writing sabbatical; thanks, guys. In addition, I would like to salute Matthew Cash, whose sound legal advice rocks my world; Laurie Levy, who got me back into writing as an adult, and helped me understand that I had something to say; and Judy Michelic, who babysat my daughter Marion when she was small—making possible the days of concentrated productivity that kept the writing thread going.

My thanks to the editors who supported my work over the years and published these and other stories in literary magazines. I will be forever grateful for the opportunity editors Jason Lee Brown and Jay Prefontaine afforded my story "Dinosaurs" when they featured it in *New Stories from the Midwest*; the anthology presented my story to a much wider audience, and also introduced me to the work of friend and colleague James Magruder. Magru, this book has benefitted from your generous gifts of time and insight. Warm thanks to friends Chris Gregoire and Mary Sustar; librarians and avid readers, they offered welcome perspective about the look of the book. And to my friends at Anderson's Bookshop in Downers Grove, IL: thank you for supporting the thinking, reading lifestyle, without which books of short stories would have no home whatsoever.

One of the greatest joys in seeing this book to its current form was the fact that treasured friends took part in its final incarnation. My warmest appreciation to John Hensler, who designed the cover of this book (and my web page). I still owe you that lunch at The Clubhouse! And to Anna Jóelsdóttir, with whom I have shared many lunches devoted to the discussion of creating, thank you for allowing your amazing artwork to grace the cover.

I am beyond grateful to Erin McKnight, Founding Editor and Publisher of Queen's Ferry Press. Erin, your support of the short

story form, and passion for writing, have been my good fortune. Thank you for your keen editing and production insights, and your belief in my work.

The Chicago-area Deals, including Violet, Cathy and Rick Segraves, Karen and Jeff Sutter, Danny, Carrie Bach, Valerie Damm, Raecel Mackrola, and their extended families, have cheered me with their support and enthusiastic attendance at readings. To the East Coast Deals—Roger, Joanie, Howie and Sara Rappaport, Michael, and Stephen: my thanks for your interest and pride, not to mention your influence at the Boylston Public Library!

My cousin Jane Marquedant Ervin's open-hearted support of, and enthusiasm for, my work have meant the world to me, and her wide-ranging reading tastes have inspired and informed my writing vision. Kevin McCoy, my old friend, you have been a champion of my work from Day One (even that story about the dog collar!), and for this I am eternally grateful. My sister Mary Kenney has kept every hard copy version of these stories that I've given her over the years; I am humbled and warmed by her staunch loyalty and pride. My brother Norman P. Kenney, his wife Brenda, and their boys Zach and Asher have provided deep support over the years, and Norm's approach to life—his many passions and interests—continue to be an inspiration to me as to how to live a full, many-faceted life and convey that breadth in my stories and characters. My mother and father, Marion and Norman A. Kenney, encouraged and celebrated that quirky sensibility in me that cropped up again and again in my life and which finally, ultimately, led me to become a writer. Would that every child had that unconditional support and love.

My husband David and daughter Marion are not only patient

with my chosen passion for writing, and the hours and distractions that passion entails, but to my everlasting gratitude, they embrace it. Marion's growth as a person provides a constant source of joy and pride. David's expertise and support as I've stepped into the world of social media has been a godsend, as has his belief in me and my work. The bond the three of us share gives me the firm center from which I can, with integrity and a clear eye, explore all the crazy, dysfunctional machinations of my characters.

Apart from the above, in the course of my life and while writing this book, I have had the privilege of meeting many people: individuals who have become dear friends, informed my days, endorsed my work, talked books and writing, and given me the gift of multiple perspectives and ways of being—every writer's dream. They are too numerous to mention here, but your unflagging support was key to the completion of this book—my sincere thanks.

I am blessed.

Stories from this book previously appeared, in slightly different form, in the following:

"Aurora" in *The Carolina Quarterly*, Vol. 58, No. 3

"Nature" in the *Ontario Review*, No. 53

"Sailor Lake" in *StoryQuarterly*, No. 34

"Phoenix" in *New Letters*, Vol. 65, No. 2

"Repo Man" in *Cutbank*, January 2010

"Dinosaurs" in *The Sun*, Issue 408. This story has also been selected for reprint; it is the lead story in an anthology from the Ohio University Press: *New Stories from the Midwest*.

Photo by John Hensler

Janice Deal's stories have appeared in literary magazines including *The Sun*, *CutBank*, the *Ontario Review*, *The Carolina Quarterly*, *StoryQuarterly*, and *New Letters*, and in the anthology, *New Stories from the Midwest*. Her collection was a finalist in the Flannery O'Connor Award for Short Fiction, and she is the recipient of an Illinois Arts Council Artists Fellowship Award for prose. *The Decline of Pigeons* is her first collection of stories to be published in book-length form. She is currently working on a novel.

Janice lives in Downers Grove, Illinois, with her husband and daughter. Learn more about her at http://janicedeal.com.

CPSIA information can be obtained at www.ICGtesting.com
Printed in the USA
BVOW040727190613

323661BV00001B/18/P